NO MATTER HOW FAR

TRINITY LAKES ROMANCE
BOOK SEVEN

SARA BETH WILLIAMS

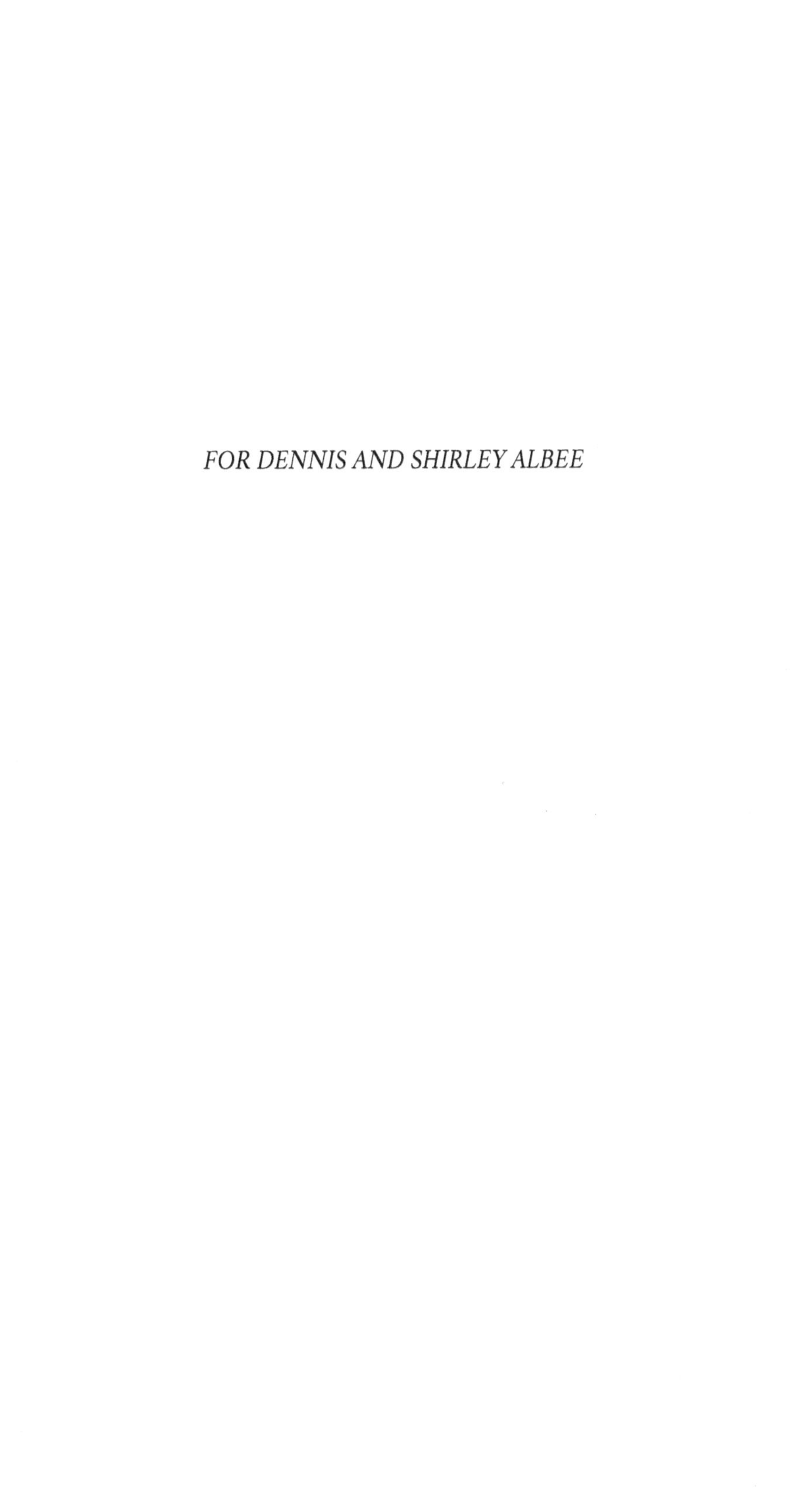

FOR DENNIS AND SHIRLEY ALBEE

Dylan Mackay set his ski poles firmly in the soft snow to keep himself from sliding down the hill. All around, snow fell soft and silent, blanketing the ski slope and cloaking the Trinity Lakes ski resort lodgings in a gray and white haze. He pulled down the scarf covering his mouth and glanced toward Ethan. "Sure this is a good idea, mate?"

Ethan grinned. "Can't turn back now, can we?" He sidled forward on his skis. "It's only a blue run. You've done this before. You'll be fine. Follow the trail markers and the rest of the skiers."

Sure, he'd done this before, years ago when he and Elise were dating, but he hadn't been back to the States in almost six years.

Come on, man. It's like riding a bike, right? He'd managed to get off the lift without falling, hadn't he?

Dylan watched Ethan push off and zigzag down the piste. The man could live on skis all year round. He should've been a ski bum instead of a theology professor at Trinity Lakes Theological Seminary. Of course, being a professor paid more. Dylan gave him that.

Dylan was content guest lecturing at Trinity Lakes Bible College, along with teaching part time as an associate professor at the seminary with Ethan. He had less responsibility than a full professor, and the pay was sufficient for his bachelorhood.

He wiped the accumulating snow from his goggles. The stuff seemed to fall faster by the minute. Loosening his poles, he used them to shove himself forward, then down the slope. Through the haze of falling snow, he zigzagged along, passing several skiers while others passed him.

He leaned right into a sharp, steep turn in the trail.

Ow!

A massive blow to his back knocked the wind out of him. He gasped for breath and tumbled forward, arms and poles outstretched to break his fall. He winced as his face hit soft, freezing snow, then cried out as something smashed into his head. He tumbled again, rolling through the snow until it coated his entire front.

He lay on his back, sucking in gulps of air. What happened? Ow. His head ached. Could he have skied over a snow-covered boulder? No, that didn't seem right. Something had knocked into his back first.

He wiped snow from his face, still gasping. He hadn't taken a tumble like that since the year Elise had taken him skiing in the States for the first time. He should call Ethan. His old mate was likely at the bottom by now.

White surrounded him, continuing to fall on his face and body. Finally able to breathe normally, he tested all his limbs, then pushed himself to a sitting position. He patted all the pockets on his coat in search of his phone. Darn, where was it this time? Had he left it back in the hotel suite? Great. Now what? Should he try to ski back down again? He rubbed his forehead and dusted snow off his front. Maybe he'd give himself five minutes to rest and try again.

That's when he noticed a dark form lying in the snow

several yards below. Fear clawed through his gut. *Oh no.* What in the world had happened?

Another skier skidded to a stop down the hill and knelt beside the figure.

Flashes of Elise lying on her side in the mud in the middle of a deserted road flickered through his mind. He closed his eyes, driving the image away with sheer will. *Please God, no waking nightmares now. Bring me peace. This isn't the same.*

For one, it'd been dreadfully humid and pouring rain, and they'd been driving down a road in the hilly regions of south-western Uganda.

Inhaling a deep breath to ward off the panic, Dylan concentrated on removing his poles and skis. The skier below removed his skis and stuck them into the snow, then spoke on his phone. Turning, he trudged up the slope toward Dylan.

"Do you know what happened?"

Dylan shook his head then winced. "Took a blow from behind. I've no idea if he hit me or what."

The other man raised his goggles and continued speaking on the phone. He wiped snow from his beanie and faced Dylan again. "You hurt at all?"

"Don't think so." He glanced at the young man lying below them on his back, cradling his arm. A snowboard lay at his feet. His own head ached, but that was nothing to fret about. "Is he okay?"

The skier ended his phone call. "Says his wrist hurts and he feels nauseous. I called the ski patrol. They should be coming to help you guys out."

Dylan nodded and waited as the other man returned to check on the snowboarder.

Wind howled through the trees as other skiers whooshed by and shot around the corner. At least they'd fallen off to the side, out of harm's way.

Snow covered Dylan's boots, pants, helmet, and beard. He

trembled as he observed the skier assist the snowboarder into a sitting position. He kept his goggles up but dusted off his beard and wrapped his face with his scarf.

The remnants of fear still clung to him, much like the all-too-frequent nightmares. He needed to stand, move around, get out of the powder he'd landed in, but he wasn't sure his legs would support him.

Two ski patrollers wearing red vests over their snow gear skidded to a stop between him and the snowboarder. While one turned and spoke to the two men below him, a young woman who looked more like a teenager turned toward him.

"Hey there." Even with skis on, she trudged uphill toward him. "I'm Renee Somers. What's your name?"

He cleared his throat and moved the scarf down from his mouth. "Dylan Mackay." He held out a gloved hand and she shook it.

"Are you hurt anywhere?" She rummaged around in her multiple coat pockets.

"I think I'm all right." Surely the other man needed more attention than him. He glanced downhill toward where the other patroller was questioning the injured man.

"Are you here with anyone?"

"My brother-in-law is around. Likely at the bottom by now."

She nodded in understanding. "You look a little cold there in the powder. Can you stand?"

She stood and held out her hand again. All right then. He'd try to stand. He grasped her hand and allowed her to help him up. The trees and the gray-white horizon tilted and spun a bit too much, and he wobbled for a second. Then he regained his balance.

Chatter from the radio on her hip confirmed a toboggan was on the way for the snowboarder. *Thank you, God.* A glance over her shoulder showed the man sitting, talking and alert. All good signs.

Renee focused on him instead of the scene behind them. "Can you tell me where you are now?"

"On a ski run at Trinity Lakes Ski Resort."

"Do you know what time of day it is?"

He squinted through the snowfall that shaded the landscape. "Midday?"

"Can you tell me what happened?"

He relayed what little information he recalled. She listened and nodded, then produced a tiny flashlight and shone it into each eye.

"So you hit your head on something, but you don't know what?"

Dylan lifted a shoulder. "He could've slammed into my head or I could've landed on my head. I'm not quite sure."

She flicked off her light, glanced back down the slope, then back at him. "You might need a toboggan, too."

He resisted the urge to rub his forehead. "I think I'll be all right if I take it slowly down the hill." The last thing he wanted was for Ethan to find him sliding down the hill on a gurney sled.

A snowmobile rumbled up the mountain toward the group, and another patroller dragging a toboggan slid down toward the snowboarder. The men in red jackets knelt around the snowboarder and continued with more questions before finally helping him sit inside the sled.

While they strapped him inside, Renee slid down the slope and spoke with the patroller on the snowmobile. Dylan carefully followed her down the slope to where they all stood together.

He caught Renee's words to the snowmobiler. "I think we should call for another toboggan."

"It's not necessary," he said before the other patroller—another woman, this one older, at least—could radio down the mountain.

The other patroller tilted her head and quirked up one side of her mouth, clearly skeptical of his statement.

"I really am okay. It'd be a waste of resources to make a second call."

The woman lifted her goggles and studied him with pretty eyes and a frustrating half-smile. "I'm Jocelyn Monroe." She offered her hand. "What's your name?"

"Dylan Mackay." He shook her hand. "Look I'm fine, truly."

"You think you know better than Renee?"

He expelled a breath and exchanged a glance with the young ski patroller in question, who waited on the side in silence, her poles anchoring her in place. Didn't patrollers have to be eighteen to be on the team? She couldn't be older than that, could she? He opened his mouth then closed it again. It wouldn't be proper to be rude to the people rescuing him.

Jocelyn glanced down the slope as her fellow patroller began his descent with the snowboarder safely aboard the gurney sled. The rest of the skiers, including the one who'd found the snowboarder and called in the ski patrol, launched off down the slope.

She returned her focus to Dylan, produced a similar penlight as Renee, and shone it in his eyes. He blinked against the bright light.

"See, no worries. I'm all right."

Renee took a step forward. "He almost fell over when he stood up."

He resisted the urge to roll his eyes like one of his college students. She had to pull that observation out, didn't she?

"Here's what I suggest." Jocelyn approached her snowmobile, removed her pack, and used the seat as a surface to unload. "We'll take some vitals, then we'll make a decision."

She proceeded to take his blood pressure, blood oxygen level, and his pulse. After she input all the readings into a tablet, she replaced everything in her bag, then slung it back over her shoulders.

"I'm perfectly all right now, see?" He stood taller, ignoring the ache that spread from his forehead to the back of his head.

"How about we compromise?" Jocelyn smiled that infuriating, luminous smile again. "You can ride on the back of my snowmobile."

He folded his arms, then glanced backward at his skis and poles sticking upward in the snow.

"We can't let you continue down the mountain in good conscience when you could have a mild concussion."

Concussion? Not likely. He was right as rain.

"Especially since Renee witnessed some dizziness."

He frowned. How irritating. Because of a single dizzy spell and a bit of a headache, he wasn't allowed to ski back down on his own?

"So it's either a sled down the hill, or a ride with me. Don't worry. We'll get your skis down the hill." She climbed aboard the snowmobile and scooted forward. "Hop on. It'll be fun."

He frowned again, inhaled a deep breath, then moved closer to the snowmobile. "All right then." What choice did he have? Ethan would never let him hear the end of it if he showed up at the bottom of the slope strapped to a toboggan.

She smiled again, and he didn't like how it did crazy things to his heart. She appeared no older than one of his college students back in Trinity Lakes.

Get a grip, man. He wasn't prone to fickle physical attraction like this. Not since Elise …

Stop. Maybe he'd hit his head harder than he'd thought.

He inhaled again and climbed onto the back behind her.

Conveniently, the snowmobile was fixed with a place to carry skis. In two minutes, Renee had snagged his wayward skis and poles and attached them to the back.

He wrapped his scarf around his face and fixed his goggles

back in place. With no other choice, unless he wanted to be flung off into the powder a second time, he hesitantly wrapped his arms around Jocelyn's waist.

The engine roared beneath him, and she turned her head to speak to him. "Hang on tight."

CHAPTER TWO

Jocelyn Monroe revved her engine and began the descent down the mountain slope. She kept to the side, watching carefully for other skiers flying past. Dylan clung to her, his warmth and the remnants of his Australian accent in her mind causing her stomach to flip like she was sixteen again.

Didn't matter how attractive he was. He was infuriatingly stubborn—typical male—and looked too old for her anyway. Though he wore that beard well.

What was wrong with her? The first man who came at her with a hot accent sends her insides tumbling? Not like she hadn't heard the accent plenty back in town. Her own church pastor had a mild Aussie accent, and several friends and acquaintances who attended also had accents. Though as far as she knew, they were all taken.

With her luck, he was already spoken for as well.

When the terrain leveled near the bottom, she sped up, spitting snow as she wove along the trail until they reached the open meadow in front of the ski lodge.

She pulled to a stop in front of the lodge and caught Renee

flying past in her peripheral vision. Dylan climbed off first, and immediately removed and inspected his skis.

All right then. No thank you or G'day to you, then. Why were so many handsome men so rude?

To the side, she spotted her boss, the head of the ski patrol, waiting in the shadow of the open doorway to the medical clinic. The scowl on Paula's face did not look welcoming.

She could shove her attitude under a rug. This man still needed a more thorough evaluation.

"Hey, Dylan?" He glanced up and his gaze connected with hers. "Come into the clinic for a minute so we can check you out in better light." And without the constant accumulation of falling snow.

He studied her as if he were about to protest. Again.

She offered her most disarming and congenial smile. Working as a paramedic for the last four years, and an EMT before that, she had practiced the ability to pacify stubborn people in the midst of a medical crisis. She'd not let him break that streak by refusing to come in for a quick exam.

"I promise it'll take ten minutes, tops. I just want to make certain you don't have a concussion or any other injury."

"Right, then." He frowned, but at least he walked toward the doorway to the first aid clinic.

Paula met him, smiled her "I'm the boss" smile, and led the way inside.

While he took off his gloves, scarf, goggles and helmet, Paula pulled Jocelyn to the side. "What in the world were you thinking taking him down on the snowmobile?" Paula asked.

Jocelyn expelled a breath. "He refused to come down in a sled. Renee and I spent ten minutes trying to figure out how to get him down without him skiing off by himself. He was showing signs of dizziness and a possible concussion. I couldn't let him ski alone."

Paula's mouth formed a thin line. "You know you can't make people accept your help."

Jocelyn didn't have time for this. She'd rather be safe now than sorry later. She pulled on a pair of latex gloves and stepped toward Dylan, then paused. Without all his gear covering his face, he looked much younger, if a little weary. Probably from tumbling down the slope. *Maybe that beanie is covering some gray hair.*

She shook the haze of attraction away, stepped toward him again, and reached both hands toward the sides of his face beneath his ears. "I've got to run through a few tests to rule out any major injuries, okay? Please bear with me."

He nodded without words, and she found she missed that accent already. She felt around the back of his ears and found no bruising. Good sign. Then she felt the vertebrate along his spine beginning at the top of his neck, checking for tenderness. Her nerves tingled in the tight proximity. When he didn't complain of any tenderness or pain, she put space between them again and breathed slowly to bring her nerves back in check.

His forehead still looked red. Gently, she ran her hand over the sore spot, her fingers brushing through the hair beneath his beanie.

"Ow."

She backed up a step and she dropped her hand.

Paula approached from the side room. "Dylan?"

He turned toward her.

"Were you skiing with someone today?"

"My friend Ethan."

"Mind if I get his contact information? We want to let him know where you are."

He rubbed his eyes and rattled off Ethan's cell number. Then Jocelyn took another round of vitals. He remained quiet and passive the entire time, as if the adrenaline from earlier had seeped out of him.

"How long have you been at the resort?"

"Today's my first day." He blinked at her. "We're here until Sunday."

He was here all week? Anticipation leapt within. *Stop it.* Realistically, she'd probably never run into him again. Hundreds of people came and went through the large resort with its plethora of slopes for all levels. After his stubborn attitude earlier, she didn't think he'd be interested in talking to her again anytime soon.

Her initial physical finished, she quickly ran through the standard concussion assessment.

Just as she finished, Paula reentered with another man behind her who she assumed must be Ethan.

Dylan turned toward them as they entered. "Where you been, mate?"

"What happened, Dylan?"

Dylan quirked up a partial smile. "Some bloke knocked me flat on the snow. Hit my head somewhere along the way. They tried to take me down in a gurney sled, but I wouldn't let 'em." He eyed Jocelyn with that half-smile that had her insides tumbling again.

Ethan took a seat in the closest chair, a clear expression of concern in his eyes. "I tried calling your phone."

He patted his sweatshirt, then turned toward his jacket, which he'd discarded.

"Bet you left it in the room. No wonder I couldn't get ahold of you."

Dylan nodded. "Didn't want to get it sopping wet."

Ethan smiled and turned toward Jocelyn. "Hey, I'm Ethan Donahue. Everything all right?"

Jocelyn removed her disposable gloves and tossed them in a nearby trash can. "He exhibited some dizziness on the mountain slope but that seems to have passed. Everything checks out right now. That helmet probably saved you from a world of trouble and pain." She tipped her head toward the blue helmet lying amid the pile of his gear on the floor.

"See. No worries." Dylan's half-smile grew, and she found it increasingly handsome with that beard.

"But concussion symptoms can take twenty-four to forty-eight hours to appear. I suggest a day of complete rest, at least."

Dylan frowned.

Ethan laughed. "First day on the slopes and you're sidelined, huh?"

Dylan shrugged, then stood and slipped his arms back in his jacket. "It is what it is."

Ethan stood and laid a hand on his shoulder. "But I'm glad nothing worse happened. Had me rattled when I couldn't find you."

Turning toward Jocelyn, Dylan offered his hand to shake. "Thanks for the ride down." His grip was warm and strong, and she found herself unable to do more than nod as he shook and released her hand before gathering the rest of his gear and tromping out of the clinic.

When they'd both left together, Paula approached her again while she cleaned and sanitized the room. "I've never known you to do something that out of protocol." She folded her arms tight and the firm scowl on her face spoke volumes. 'I don't care how cute he is. No more passengers on your snowmobile. Got it?"

Who said anything about cute? Had she said something aloud? Was it that obvious? She kept her gaze away from Paula, lest the cranky woman read her thoughts in her expression. "Won't happen again."

But would she truly do it again, despite Paula's warning? Maybe. Or maybe Dylan's accent really was that alluring.

———

DYLAN LOUNGED on the couch in their shared hotel suite. He should be in bed. "I'm ruined, mate."

Ethan laughed as he pulled a plate holding some kind of frozen meal from the microwave. "Because you're losing a day of skiing or because you're exhausted?" He found a can of soft drink in the mini fridge. "I can't believe you spilled like that on the first day. What're you going to do all day tomorrow?"

Dylan kicked a leg up onto the coffee table. "You mean you're not going to sit with me and binge movies all day? Thought we came here to hang together?"

Ethan shook his head, still laughing. "You're on your own."

Dylan frowned. Of course Ethan would choose the slopes over his old pal. He shouldn't have expected anything different. Ethan would choose the slopes over his own mother. "You invited me, you know."

"You could just chuck the pretty lady's warnings and ski anyway."

"Better not to risk it." His head still hurt, and exhaustion clung to him like a wet blanket.

"She said you don't even have a concussion." Ethan brought his meal to the couch. "She was pretty, though. What was her name again?"

Dylan opened his mouth to answer, then shut it tight. No sense in encouraging the bloke to keep going. He'd spent less than an hour with her, after all. Regardless of her attractive smile and the compassionate care she'd given, he'd likely not see her again.

"Says the engaged man over there." Honestly, it was a wonder Ethan worked at the seminary. Dylan didn't recall him acting like this during all the years he and Elise were together.

Maybe it was the brother-brother dynamic. Brothers acted

differently around each other than they did sisters. Sure, he was less crass around his three sisters back in Sydney.

Maybe Ethan was nervous about being tied down in marriage.

Dylan frowned. Not a great sign. He'd seen plenty of Lillian since August and couldn't come up with one complaint about her.

"Nah, man, I wasn't talking about me." Ethan raised his eyebrows as he shoveled a load of veggies into his mouth.

Dylan scowled and brought his leg down off the table. "Don't play matchmaker with me, Ethan. I don't want your help."

Ethan had the decency to look repentant, but he continued to eat in infuriating silence, as if waiting for Dylan to say more. Well, he could wait all night. Dylan wasn't about to play this game. He pushed himself up to stand. Ow, ouch. Some pain meds would help. And sleep.

"Come on, Dylan. Don't walk away like that."

Dylan said not a word as he entered the shared hall bathroom to find a bottle of pain meds.

Ethan followed. "Dylan, Elise has been gone for nearly four years."

He shook his head, then regretted that decision as his headache intensified.

"Dylan."

He left the bathroom and then found his suitcase. Rummaging through the pockets, he finally found the packet of pain medication he'd packed. Good. Standing, he found himself face to face with Ethan.

"At least acknowledge that she is pretty. And kind. And helpful."

Anger sparked in his chest. "If you invited me all the way to the States just to set me up with another American, then I'm keen to fly right back home again."

Ethan blinked and frowned, and a pang of guilt shot through

Dylan. His mate was getting married next summer. He'd suggested Dylan visit for the year leading up to the wedding and had even secured him a position at the seminary. Dylan was being rude, and Ethan didn't deserve any of it.

But the anger wouldn't loosen, as hard as he tried to breathe deep.

Elise was gone. Ethan was right. His wife was long gone.

That didn't mean he wanted to find a replacement.

"I invited you here because I knew you were stuck. Grieving for years and going nowhere. You needed a fresh start." Ethan folded his arms, his usual levity dissipating. "But maybe it's too soon."

Dylan scowled. The hint of sarcasm in Ethan's tone didn't match his half-apology. Gripping the pain meds, Dylan made for the door of the suite. His head ached something fierce. He'd find a restroom in the lounge or swallow the pills without water. Anything to create distance.

Before he could get out the door, Ethan laid a hand on his shoulder. "I'm sorry. That wasn't fair. I loved Elise, and I miss her too. She was my only sister."

The uncharacteristic waver in the voice of the guy who laughed and joked around about everything brought a ball of emotion up Dylan's throat.

Ethan dropped his hand. "But at some point, it will be time to move on."

Dylan bolted down the hall until he found an alcove. There, he choked down two pills and leaned back against the wall.

What do you think, God?

He chided himself for asking a stupid question. God had been egging him to move on as much as Ethan and his family back home had. Except what God wanted him to do was far more daunting than what Ethan and his family wanted of him.

Maybe he should listen. Maybe he should go back to Africa.

Maybe he could … if not for the strangling fear that woke

him in the form of nightmares at least once a week. Reliving the car crash that injured Elise and resulted in her death was exhausting.

Now You want me to go back?

He shook his head. He could not—would not again—take another wife into the mission field.

CHAPTER THREE

A warm aroma of bacon and sausage filled the resort's main restaurant. Jocelyn loaded her plate from the breakfast buffet line with way too much food, but she didn't care. She had an entire day to herself on the mountain. She'd burn off all the carbs in no time.

She scanned the packed room, conversation rising and falling like rushing water. A familiar face stared back at her from a corner table near the huge two-story windows overlooking the bunny hill runs.

He sat alone. And somehow, he appeared more handsome than ever in a thick forest green sweater. And no gray in that soft, natural-looking, light brown hair that stuck up in odd places.

No gray whatsoever.

She found herself drawn to him, against her better judgment.

Last night, Renee had cornered her at dinner and gushed about the guy's amazing accent, and didn't Jocelyn think it gorgeous too? Then she'd gone and mentioned that the man had a brother-in-law. But Jocelyn hadn't seen a ring when he'd taken off his gloves.

She eyed his right hand.

No ring.

Maybe some guys didn't wear rings? Maybe he was separated? Divorced? Or maybe the brother-in-law was his sister's husband?

She cleared her throat as she approached with her tray, even though he'd tracked her progress across the restaurant. "Mind if I sit with you?"

"Didn't expect to see you again." He lifted a hand, showing the chair across from him, and studied her as she set down her plate of food. "You eating for two, or planning on running a marathon?" He flashed a quirky smile.

"I've got the day off, and I'd planned to ski half the mountain."

"Well, that explains it." He shoved a bite of sausage in his mouth and chewed before continuing. "Lucky you."

She ate, studying him as she did. He appeared well and alert this morning, less grumpy even. All good signs.

"Did Ethan ditch you?"

"Right, he did." Dylan frowned and drank from a glass of orange juice. He finished off his biscuit. "Lucky I ran into you though. I considered checking out the snowmobile tours, then thought maybe I should run it by the patrol first."

She laughed. "It's okay. You don't have to check in with us." But his teasing smile and the spark in his eyes said he just might be flirting with her.

"But I still want to know." He wiped his mouth with a napkin. "Do you think it's a good idea? After all, you recommended a complete day of rest."

She mulled over his request as she finished her scrambled eggs.

"Might be safer if you came with me. To make sure I really

don't have a concussion after all." He grinned, his gaze connecting with hers.

Was he *flirting* with her? And asking her out?

He finished off the last sausage on his plate. "Of course, if I'm being too presumptuous and you've got your day all planned, then—"

"I have to ask you something first."

He sat back, waiting.

"Are you married?"

His smile vanished, but he didn't break eye contact.

Oh, she'd hit a nerve. Should she have asked? Was it too soon? Too personal a question? She continued eating while he sat in contemplation.

He rubbed his chin and fixed his gaze out the window beside them. "I used to be married, yes. Not anymore."

She ate one of her two biscuits, and he sat still, waiting on her. She bit her lip. "You're single? Honest?"

"Honest." Half his mouth quirked upward. "And you?"

"I am as well." She nodded and ate another bite.

"Now that that's squared away." He rested one arm across the back of the empty chair next to him. "Do you think it's safe for me to go snowmobiling?"

She ate another two mouthfuls of scrambled eggs. "I'm sure you'd exert much less energy snowmobiling than any other activity. Might be a good choice."

He grinned now. "See, that's what I was thinking. And no doubt you know the trails well." He leaned toward her. "So, are you free today?"

She stifled a giggle at his smile and the spark in his eyes. She drank the rest of her glass of juice, purposefully pushing away the information that all snowmobile tours were led by an experienced guide. If he thought she could be his guide, who was she to argue?

"Let's meet in fifteen then, and I'll show you where we can rent snowmobiles."

Still grinning, he said, "It's a date."

———

DYLAN'S HEART hammered hard as he trudged through the snow behind Jocelyn toward the snowmobiling trailhead.

Last night, his head had been in the clouds, but he'd shrugged off his attraction. Surely, it'd been all the rush of adrenaline and hitting his head too hard. He'd fully expected to wake up with all of the instant infatuation gone from his system.

Then he'd seen her walk into the restaurant, bright-eyed and beautiful, and everything had come rushing back. How equally stubborn she'd been, standing up to him. How it felt to hold onto her while they rode down the mountain. How gentle and kind she'd been during her examination.

What was he thinking, asking to spend the day with her? He knew exactly three things about this woman—she worked as a paramedic, her name was Jocelyn, and she loved to ski. Four things, if he counted that she loved eating a bucketload and working it off afterward.

What am I doing? She could live across the country and he'd never see her again after this week.

Then again, he lived halfway across the world. Though he planned to reside in Trinity Lakes for the foreseeable future.

Did she attend church? Did she even care about religion? What all would she have to say about him teaching biblical and theological studies?

What if she were dating someone else?

No, she'd indicated she was single already.

So, he knew five things about her.

Six. She could drive a snowmobile with precision.

Seven. Her long hair blowing in the wind made her beautiful.

She really didn't know him either. He'd neglected to indicate he was widowed. Wouldn't that have been an automatic mood killer?

Yet she'd agreed to be with him today. That had to mean something.

God, what am I doing?

A stab of guilt knifed through him at the realization that he'd not once consulted with the One who held everything in His hands before making this rash decision.

"Here we are," she said over her shoulder as they approached a garage-like structure where multiple snowmobiles were parked in a line.

They each paid their rental fees and waited while the trail guide and instructor explained how the snowmobiles operated. Of course, he spent more time showing Dylan what to do, as Jocelyn already knew her way around a snowmobile.

"Joss, you've done this trail multiple times. Do you need me leading the way?" The instructor, whose nametag read Dan, smiled at Jocelyn with familiarity.

She laughed and shook her head, then glanced at Dylan. "Only if you're okay with me leading instead?"

Dylan offered a shrug. The sun shone bright from a gorgeous, clear blue sky. Yesterday, he'd ridden on the back of hers while she drove down a steep slope through heavy snowfall. If the instructor trusted her, he would too.

"But I'll take a radio if you have a spare. In case we run into trouble."

Dan nodded, left, and returned with a walkie-talkie, then they chatted more about the conditions of the trail, and reviewed the safety information and places to avoid.

Finally settled on their snowmobiles, Jocelyn led the way along the flat landscape. The rumbling engines echoed as they glided through fields of glistening white. The concoction of unease and anticipation of being alone together with a woman for the first time in years settled into a feeling of tentative tranquility. The sheer beauty of the wilderness landscape surrounding him overpowered the initial attraction that seemed to turn his brain into cotton whenever he was in her presence.

Jocelyn led him through wide open trails where sunlight spilled through tall pines and spruces, their branches still dusted with snow from yesterday's storm. The tall trees cast long shadows across the snow. For a time, they saw not another soul as they rumbled along. When she pulled to a stop, he glided up next to her and followed suit.

She turned off her snowmobile, lifted her goggles, dug a bottle of water from her backpack, and tossed it to him.

"Thanks."

She smiled, her long hair flowing down her shoulders. "What do you think so far?"

He surveyed the beauty around him as a serene hush of silence fell. The warmth of the sun shone through a break in the pines to their left. The woosh of wind through branches and the occasional bird call were the only disturbances. "It's absolutely gorgeous."

She grinned. "Helps that the weather is perfect today."

"That it is."

"How are you feeling so far?"

He smiled and tapped the helmet protecting his head. "Just fine."

"I'm glad." She dug a hair tie from her pack and pulled back her hair into a ponytail. She pulled two muesli bars from her backpack and offered one to him.

He declined for now. He couldn't fathom how she could still be hungry, but he smiled nonetheless.

"Did you learn to ski in the States or in Australia?"

Dylan drank from his water bottle, taking time to carefully form his thoughts without bringing Elise into it. "I learned in the States years ago, but yeah, I have been skiing in Australia. It is an experience unlike any other."

She raised her brows. "How so?"

"For starters, we ski through gum trees or boulders instead of pines." He gestured to the towering pines surrounding them. "It's a different atmosphere altogether."

Jocelyn led them up an incline along another wide trail that wove through the forest. It narrowed significantly at one point, then widened as they crested the top of a hill. There, Jocelyn stopped again and cut her engine. He did the same.

In the distance, three lakes, one larger than the others, could be seen through a narrow break in the trees. "Looks like Trinity Lakes."

"That's right." She glanced sideways at him, her orange goggles reflecting the picturesque environment around them. "Only a short drive down the mountain."

Lake Wainscott, the largest, shone a sparkling dark blue against the backdrop of gray mountain peaks and dark green woods.

The question of where she was from hung on the tip of his tongue, but he hesitated. Was this something he wanted to pursue past this week? He'd been the one to ask her out on impulse, but did he want to take it beyond five or six days?

Was he brave enough?

"Have you visited Trinity Lakes?" she asked.

Looks like she beat you to it, mate.

He inhaled and nodded. "Ethan has a place there, on the north side of the lake. That's where I'm staying."

"Really?" She lifted her goggles and her wide eyes shone with excited surprise. "I'm from Trinity Lakes, too. I live on the southern side."

His stomach tightened with anticipation. "Really?" It couldn't be, could it?

Beaming, she nodded and leaned forward on her snowmobile, closer toward him. "I grew up there, then attended college in California, and returned about five years ago. I attend church there, and work as a paramedic while I'm finishing my nursing degree. This is my third winter volunteering with the ski patrol, and I also volunteer with a mountain search and rescue team."

This woman amazed him. He couldn't help but stare.

She checked her time on her smartwatch. "We should head back and maybe grab something to eat."

"You're still hungry after eating a breakfast fit for three?" He laughed. If only he had the metabolism of a twenty-something again. Unfortunately, his dropped when he'd hit thirty.

She laughed too, struggling to reschool her features before readjusting her goggles over her eyes again. "We haven't seen a lot of people so far, but we'll be going parallel to a beginner trail in a little bit here, and we'll see plenty of skiers and snow-boarders on the side."

He nodded, drank the rest of his water, and followed her again as they entered the beginner piste.

CHAPTER FOUR

Late the next evening, after a long day on patrol, Jocelyn found herself at dinner in the restaurant surrounded by the volunteer ski patrol squad. Most patrons had eaten and had either left for home or returned to their rooms at the resort's hotel across the parking lot. Different cliques of patrollers had returned at separate times after final checks around the entire park, and now most of them sat spread across the large room, laughing and decompressing from their day as they ate.

Renee giggled and her elbow connected with Jocelyn's side. "So, you went snowmobiling together, just the two of you? Alone?"

"I should never have told you." Jocelyn shoveled a forkful of spaghetti into her mouth.

Jesse Hernandez, another long-time volunteer ski patrol and SAR team member, sat on the other side of the table. He cut a sharp glance toward Jocelyn. "Wait, who did you go off into the wilderness with all alone?"

Jocelyn frowned at Renee. Why did she have to say anything aloud? Who she spent time with alone was no one else's business.

Renee smiled at Jesse. "Some guy she rescued from the top of the ski slope on Monday."

Jocelyn rolled her eyes while she ate. *Here we go.*

Jesse snickered. "Is that so?" He forked a big bite of spaghetti in his mouth to cover an obvious laugh.

Ignoring her half-eaten plate of food, Renee turned to face Jocelyn. "So he said he was married? But not anymore? And he's here with his brother-in-law?"

She nodded as she ate another bite of pasta. That about summed it up.

"Doesn't that seem odd to you? What divorced guy hangs out with his ex's brother?"

"It's not any of my business to ask what drama went down." She bit into a piece of French bread. They weren't in a relationship. Renee insinuating that today's outing constituted a date was a stretch.

Dylan would tell her what happened in his own time.

"Maybe he's lying." Jesse's straight face tugged Jocelyn's mouth downward.

Renee ate a bite of salad. "To who, though?"

Jesse stared hard at Jocelyn and pointed his fork at her.

She shook her head. "He doesn't seem like the lying type." She would know. She dated a liar for two years too long. She chewed, mulling over that.

She'd like to think she had much better judgment of character now, but maybe she wouldn't know. If she'd been more perceptive, she wouldn't have dated the last lying ex in the first place.

Jesse shrugged and continued eating. "Could be it's his sister's husband."

Jocelyn shook her head no again. She hadn't seen a ring on the other guy's finger when he'd met Dylan in the clinic. But maybe they didn't like wearing rings? Some people didn't.

Renee snapped her fingers. "Future brother-in-law! Maybe he just neglected the word 'future'".

"Could be his wife died. How old is he anyway?"

Jocelyn froze with her fork halfway to her mouth. What a morbid thought. She truly hoped Jesse's assumption was wrong.

Renee shrugged and resumed eating. "Old enough to treat me like I was a child." She laughed, as she always did. "Maybe in his thirties or something."

Jesse pursed his lips, concern in his eyes. "It doesn't bother you?"

Renee smiled, chewed, then answered. "I have a baby face and it's something I'm used to. You know that already."

"That shouldn't be an excuse for people to treat you with disrespect."

Jocelyn frowned, tuning their conversation out. Full beards played tricks when it came to perception of age. Maybe Dylan was younger than he looked. She could check the chart records at the clinic to verify his age. Tomorrow she'd make a point to do so. If he didn't just tell her his age first.

Jocelyn finished and waved as she left the table. The idea that Dylan had lied to her didn't sit well in her stomach. *Somehow, I have to get him to tell me what happened in the past.* But how could she do that tactfully without ruining their very-new-and-thoroughly exhilarating friendship?

The next morning at breakfast, she found him sitting alone again in the same spot. Today he wore a thick, deep gray sweater. This time, she limited the amount of food she piled on her plate. Though his teasing made her stomach flip, she didn't want to seem like she ate like a linebacker on a regular basis.

He smiled as she approached. "Deciding to cut back today, are you?"

She couldn't hold in her laughter. "Is that the first thing you noticed, the amount of food on my plate?"

His eyes flashed with intensity and heat rushed up her neck. No, apparently, that was not the first thing he'd noticed.

She deliberately ignored the inclination to ask, sat and began eating. Now … how to approach the topic of his past marriage. Should she just ask him outright? Or use more subtle questioning?

He drank from his glass of orange juice. "I overslept and Ethan ditched me again."

She raised her eyebrows. "Oh?" Was that true, or was he here, trying to orchestrate a meeting with her?

"I'm sure he's risking his life on some double black diamond somewhere. He tried to take me on one, but I refused."

Jocelyn tried not to laugh as she ate. She'd be out doing the same thing. "Is he like that often, risking his life?" Did she know him? She'd been back in town for a while, but the name and face didn't ring any bells. She rifled through all the memorable emergency calls and mountain rescues she'd done but had no recollection of the man she'd seen with Dylan at the clinic. If he were an avid outdoorsman, he'd never been rescued or involved in an emergency.

"He's calmed some, I think, over the years." Dylan shrugged.

Oh! So, they'd known each other for a while, then?

"What does his wife think?" *Perfect.* Subtle. Not nosy or prying.

"He's engaged at the moment." Dylan gazed out the large window and rubbed his beard. "That's a good question, though. I should ask Lillian what she thinks." He cracked a smile, as if anticipating that conversation.

"Is Lillian your sister?"

He shook his head, laughter sparking in his eyes. "No. I only met her in August. Nice woman."

And he wasn't Dylan's sister's husband.

Which brought her back to square one. How to ask the hard, prying questions.

She cleared her throat and opted for something else entirely. "What're your plans this morning?"

He lifted a shoulder. "I'm here to ski, so ..."

"Have you ever tried cross-country skiing?"

He shook his head.

"Would you like to try?"

He lifted his shoulder again, flashing that dashing smile that she couldn't get out of her head since they'd parted the day before. "Might be fun to try something new. You're off today, then?"

She smiled, struggling to keep her excitement at bay. What was it about this man that made her want to drop everything and spend every second with him?

"How often do you patrol?"

"Tomorrow's my last day volunteering for this week. I usually volunteer one day off, one day on, and stay for a week or so at a time at the beginning and end of the season."

He nodded. "Meet you outside then in a bit when you're ready?"

Half an hour later, they stood outside together with their skis on, and she ran through the basics of cross-country skiing. Then she led him to the entrance to the cross-country ski trail on the other side, across from the beginner ski lift that led up the mountain.

He caught on quickly, shuffling and gliding alongside her with little trouble. She smiled as she watched him push forward, staying parallel with her.

"Pretty good for an old man." She laughed.

He cut a sharp glance in her direction. "Is thirty-four old in the States?" His teeth shone bright through his beard as he smiled.

Finally, an age. Thirty-four. All right. She expelled a breath, nerves tumbling in her stomach as they continued together along the paved track. In the summer, green meadows filled with wildflowers surrounded these popular hiking trails. Now, a serene blanket of snow covered everything under a gray sky that promised more snow to come.

They pushed on across the flat ground, shuffling and gliding together. A gondola gliding on a line above them caught her eye. She grinned as she tracked its progress.

Dylan paused beside her and glanced upward. "That looks clever."

She squinted at him. "Huh?"

"Looks like fun," he amended.

A second gondola passed overhead, following the other on the mechanical line. "It's one of my favorite things to do at the resort."

During her childhood, she'd heard rumors that some long-ago developer had wanted to extend the gondola lines all the way down and across Lake Wainscott, but the development project had been blocked somehow. Having a gondola travel over the wilderness down to the lake would've been breathtaking. Of course, she had no clue what other ideas the developer had had planned that might have been detrimental to the small-town atmosphere of Trinity Lakes.

Dylan studied her for a moment, silent and contemplative. Odd. But she turned and pushed off again.

The longer they glided along, the more her nerves churned. *I have to figure out the truth, or it's going to drive me crazy.* She finally found a good place to stop, off the track near a wooden picket fence, out of the way of others who might be on the trail this morning. Opening her backpack, she pulled out two water bottles and handed him one. He smiled his thanks.

"Can I ask you something?"

He took a drink, then nodded. "Ask away."

She closed her eyes and inhaled deeply. Now, how could she go about this tactfully? She opened her eyes and lifted her goggles in order to make eye contact. "You said you used to be married. What happened?"

He lifted his goggles and his gaze collided with hers, his green eyes bright and intense. Unlike yesterday, he didn't hesitate. "My wife died almost four years ago."

She expelled a breath she hadn't known she'd been holding. Jesse had been right. She covered her mouth, the apology she desperately wanted to voice caught in an emotional clog in her throat. How awful and how sad.

He turned toward the snow-covered meadow and leaned against the wooden fencing. "She was from Trinity Lakes. We married after I graduated from Trinity Lakes Theological Seminary. Ethan and I met and became friends first, and then he introduced me to her." He paused and took another drink of water before continuing. "After Elise and I married, I applied for dual citizenship before we …" He cleared his throat. "But after she died …" He paused again, as if reflecting. "I went back to Australia for a while to be with my family, since I hadn't seen them in years."

Her boots crunched over the snow as she moved closer and leaned on the fence next to him, careful to keep herself from bumping into him. Things were already awkward and emotional enough.

"Why didn't you say anything?" She covered her mouth again. "I'm sorry. That was rude." She turned away and faced the trail. What was wrong with her? They barely knew each other. Maybe it wouldn't have been out of line if they were actually dating. But to call this a 'relationship' was wishful thinking. Of course, he wouldn't want to talk about a deceased wife. Now his earlier secrecy made sense.

"It's all right, Jocelyn."

She snuck a glance back toward him and found a sort of sad smile on his face.

"It's not something you bring up over breakfast." His smile grew slightly. "Anyhow, it was long ago."

But the sadness in his eyes contradicted the casual tone of his voice. Her death might have been years ago, but what if part of him wasn't quite over her yet?

33

CHAPTER FIVE

They made the rest of the trek back to the main lodge in relative silence, but Dylan could tell this news hadn't been expected. Which is why he hadn't brought it up at all. They needed to talk it out more. Was he prepared to talk about who he once had been? What he and Elise had been together? All the experiences they'd shared?

It all seemed like another life. Could it really have been less than six years since he'd lived in Uganda with Elise, helping to spread God's word? While the memories were often clear, the timeline of events felt completely skewed.

When they arrived back at the ski rental shop, they both bent down to remove their cross-country skis so they could return them.

His phone vibrated against his chest, and he pulled it from his pocket. Ethan.

You up for a few runs together before I head back to see my parents for dinner?

That's right. Today was Thanksgiving. Ethan had invited him to eat with his family tonight, as his parents lived in a mountain cabin not far down the road. Given the rollercoaster emotional state he'd been in all week, Dylan had declined.

As long as we stay off the black and double black diamonds.

Fine, fine.

Too many memories of him and Elise during the holidays swirled inside, like the white snowflakes in the sky above. He couldn't allow himself to sink into memories and what ifs and regrets. Not now.

Jocelyn had already moved up the line to the rental shop's reception window.

"Jocelyn." He caught up to her, ignoring the people behind him. She turned to face him, and he studied her guarded expression. "Are you leaving tomorrow night after work?"

She shook her head. "Ski patrol days are long. I prefer driving the mountain roads in daylight, so I usually don't leave until the next morning."

"I'm heading off to meet with Ethan now, but ... will you meet me by the hearth tonight, downstairs in the main lodge? After eight?"

She tilted her head, staring off into the distance where they held ski and snowboard lessons on a flat, open field of white. Then she cut her glance back at him. "Okay."

That night, after dark, Dylan arrived in the main lodge's lounge to a roaring fire in the huge brick-laid hearth. No one else sat in the foyer, and the restaurant across the way was half as full as he'd seen it in days past. Could be the later hour. Could be the holiday had lured people home to their families.

Now he waited, his stomach in knots. *God, what would you have me do with this amazing woman?* He'd been walking—or skiing—in a dreamland all day, so much so that Ethan had quickly taken note. The incessant teasing hadn't helped settle his nerves.

The longer he waited by the fire, the more his anticipation morphed into doubt. Was his perception of their chemistry way off base? Had he scared her off with the whole, "my wife died" bit?

Then she glided through the lobby doors, surveyed the lounge, and approached with a tired smile on her beautiful face. The heaviness and unease from earlier had dissipated from her demeanor and he exhaled in relief.

"I'm sorry." She breathed hard, then sat beside him on the small couch. "My brother called to say hi for Thanksgiving, and then a minor medical emergency occurred on my floor, so I helped walk a woman to her car so they could get to the hospital down the mountain."

"Wow, really?"

"The life of a paramedic." She expelled a heavy breath, then shed her winter coat to reveal a thick pale pink sweater, with one of those puffy never-ending scarves of the same color circling her neck. "Sometimes I feel like I'm never off duty."

"I can only imagine." He held his chin in his hand. "You mentioned you're in school for nursing?"

She nodded and smiled this dream-like smile, a smile filled with aspiration, hope, and light, a smile he wanted to memorize and never forget. "Someday I would love to volunteer in medical missions overseas."

She was interested in working overseas? He blinked, simultaneously in awe and frightened by the sheer coincidence.

She continued speaking, oblivious to the swinging pendulum of his emotions. "Or I'd love to work as a flight medic. Either option will take a lot of work experience to get there. Flight medic positions can be extremely competitive."

He smiled, totally enamored. Indeed, she had high aspirations, and he had no doubt she'd achieve them if she put her heart into it. "Both admirable goals."

"Thanks." She smiled a shy endearing smile. "For now, I'm focused on graduating, and then passing this big nursing exam I have to take afterward."

"How old are you?"

"Twenty-nine."

"Are you still volunteering for search and rescue?"

She shook her head. "I volunteered until June of last year, but I had so many clinical nursing hours that conflicted with my SAR responsibilities, and I expected the workload this semester to be intense, so I resigned from the team. But I'm thinking of rejoining."

He nodded. Understandable.

"How much longer are you staying at the resort?"

He pulled himself out of the haze he'd fallen into. "We'd planned to leave early Sunday morning. And you?"

"I'm debating whether to stay an extra day and ski on Saturday." She leaned back into the corner of the couch and crossed one leg over the other. "But I've got free lodging while volunteering with the patrol."

They talked more about skiing, and she mentioned again that she'd grown up in Trinity Lakes, spent much of her childhood here at the resort all year round, until she left for college at eighteen.

"What brought you back to town?"

The brightness in her eyes dimmed and her gaze drifted away from his. The fire crackled in the background while he waited for her to form her thoughts.

"When I was twenty-four, my parents split without warning. Shook our world." She wrapped her arms around her middle. "Afterward, my mom just … left. My younger brother had already left the state two years before. That left my dad all alone. So, I returned to stay with him. And then …" Her eyes misted and she ran a finger beneath each one. "Less than a year later, he died of a heart attack."

Dylan reached for her hand, and she didn't resist. He knew all too well that awful, terrible, and all-encompassing feeling of loss. "Is that what inspired you to pursue becoming a nurse?"

"I'd had a background as a medical receptionist but after that experience, I applied to become an EMT. Then I became a paramedic as soon as I could get the certification. Then I looked into nursing programs."

His heart expanded in growing affection. Where he'd run away and hid from his calling, she'd run toward the very situations that had brought on the loss of her father.

She checked the time on her watch. "I've got an early morning. I should go." She gathered her jacket in her arms.

He stood when she stood. "Can I walk you back to your room?"

She nodded and led the way toward the second story covered walkway that connected the main lodge and hotel.

As they walked down the hall, heat blasting from vents above, he reached for her hand again. She remained quiet, except when giving directions.

"You're very brave, you know that." He squeezed her hand.

"Thanks." She pushed hair out of her face and attempted a wobbly smile. "And thanks for listening."

He shoved his free hand in his pocket and ran his thumb over her knuckles with his other. "Sometimes I wish I could do what you've done. Facing your fears every day."

In front of her doorway, he turned toward her. "My wife and I were missionaries in Uganda together for a year and a half. We were driving on a road toward one of the remote villages when another car came barreling toward us. I had to swerve to avoid a head-on collision." His throat felt as raw as sandpaper as he pushed on. "The other car roared off while we ended up sliding into a tree. I was conscious enough and able to get out, but Elise was thrown from the car."

He closed his eyes as images of Elise landing in the middle of the road flickered through his mind.

Without him realizing, Jocelyn released his hand, wrapped

her arms around him and leaned against him in a warm embrace. "I'm sorry, Dylan. That's awful."

"No more awful than what you went through." He relished the warmth of her embrace only for a moment before he stepped back and shoved both hands into his pockets lest he run them through that long hair and bring her closer still.

"Can we meet again tomorrow night? Same place? After I get off patrol?"

He nodded and stepped back. "I'd like that."

"Can I text you?"

He sucked in a breath but kept himself composed well enough as he dipped his chin. She pulled out her phone, and he rattled off his number.

Later, as he walked back to his room, he stared at the text she sent him.

I had a blast today. Don't be a stranger.

He closed his eyes against a wave of grief. How long had it been since he'd gotten another woman's phone number? He pocketed his phone and silently let himself into the room to prepare for bed.

CHAPTER SIX

Jocelyn heaved deep breaths as she flew down the mountain, snow spitting behind her as she wove through unsuspecting skiers who were oblivious to the harrowing emergency unfolding below.

She had to get there now. *Lord, please don't let us be too late.*

She skidded to a stop in front of a fallen snowboarder and two other teary-eyed friends. This call would be the one she remembered long after the week ended.

A teenage girl stood above the fallen snowboarder, her knees bent, still strapped to her board, tears in her eyes. "He keeps coming in and out."

He was only a kid. Maybe eleven. No helmet. Or maybe it'd flown off. Jocelyn kneeled next to him and tapped him hard on the shoulder, listening for any kind of response whatsoever. "Hey, can you hear me?"

When he groaned, she let out a long breath. She hastily unzipped his jacket, then felt along the neck until she could feel a pulse. It was slow, but present. Unzipping her pack, she retrieved a portable blood pressure cuff and blood oxygen monitor.

She cut a fleeting glance toward the other girl. "What's his name?"

"Aiden."

Again, she tapped his shoulder and called his name, praying for a response. She studied his eyes, and they blinked rapidly then closed again. She quickly removed his gloves, rolled up his sleeves, and attached her tools to obtain his vitals.

Jesse skidded to a stop, spitting snow behind him, breathing heavy. "Do you need anything?"

"I need a spine board, splints, at least two more patrollers, a toboggan, and get Paula on the line."

Aiden groaned and his breathing became labored. He needed an airlift out of here. Now.

Radio chatter echoed from her walkie-talkie as Jesse made the calls she'd requested. She turned toward Jesse. "Clear the entire slope."

He nodded and radioed the lifts above then below. While he did that, she spoke with the boy's friends, and gathered as much information as possible about what happened prior to his fall. She monitored his blood pressure and blood oxygen with mounting trepidation.

Once he got ahold of Paula on the radio, Jocelyn spoke rapidly. "We need a helo medical evac ASAP. I've got an eleven-year-old male, in and out of consciousness, with labored breathing."

As they spoke, three other patrollers arrived with the equipment she'd requested.

"Can you get him down the mountain to flatter ground?" Paula asked over the radio.

"I'll try and let you know if I can't."

Jesse rested a hand on her shoulder. "The lifts are closed for this run." She nodded her thanks.

With extreme caution, the team of patrollers lifted him onto the spine board, strapped him down tight, then lifted and slid him into the toboggan. After securing him in, they all as one skied down the mountain toward flatter ground.

Jocelyn heard the helicopter before she saw it, its blades echoing over the sea of evergreens.

Where the slope flattened, they all slowed to a stop and waited while flight medics disembarked and took over. Jocelyn filled them in on everything she knew while the wind of the blades whooshed overhead.

Once they'd loaded the boy into the chopper, two patrollers escorted the remaining teens down the mountain. Radio chatter filled her walkie-talkie.

Jesse stood beside her as the aircraft lifted off into the blue sky above.

"You still want to do that?" He turned to face her, gesturing toward the departing helicopter. "Be a flight medic?"

She smiled. "Maybe someday." Her heart raced at high speed. Her stomach churned and she mouthed a prayer. *Lord, be with this kid. Help him hang on.*

"Are you planning on volunteering with the SAR team in the New Year?"

"Hoping to."

"Oh, you should come rock climbing with me at the adventure park. Pick a weekend. I'll pay your way. It'll be good practice."

She nodded, watching the helicopter fly over the tops of the trees.

"Jocelyn." Paula's voice crackled over the radio.

"Here."

"You good or do you need a break?"

Annoyance reared up within, but she tamped it down. "I'm okay. I promise."

She never could sit around and wallow after a difficult crisis. Being in the midst of helping others, keeping people safe, and successfully saving lives took away the sting, kept her mind busy, and her adrenaline pumping. If she took a break any time a major crisis occurred, her adrenaline would wane, and she'd find herself completely exhausted for the rest of the day.

That night, after clearing the last of the stragglers off the runs and then filling out incident reports, Jocelyn met up with the rest of the staff in the restaurant to eat together. But her adrenaline waned faster than usual, and she couldn't forget the half-conscious face of that snowboarder.

Had she done enough? Had she assessed him correctly and made the right call? Had they been extra careful spine-boarding him? Had they gotten him down the mountain and into the chopper fast enough?

Most of the others who had responded to that call appeared melancholy and conversation remained minimal. Jesse ducked out earlier than usual but bent to give her a quick hug.

"See you when I see you." His typical farewell. "Scratch that. I'll see you at your graduation."

She smiled. "Are you leaving tomorrow?"

"In the morning. As much as I'd love to stay, I'm still working at the adventure park."

"There's a ski instructor position opening at the resort."

He exhaled a breath and shook his head. "I love working at the resort, but this job is full time and year-round."

She nodded. Made sense.

"What about you? Leaving tomorrow?" He flashed a half smile, a bit of mischief in his eyes.

She tore her gaze away and poked at her half-eaten chicken. "Not sure yet." She'd love to spend another day on the slopes with Dylan.

His expression sobered. "You made the right call today, Joss. Remember that."

After everyone at her table left, Jocelyn eyed the lobby area near the huge hearth. Bright, warm firelight and the image of Dylan's handsome smile in her mind's eye coaxed her toward the collection of high-end couches covered in blankets and huge pillows.

She leaned into one of the pillows and checked the time on her phone. After eight, and Dylan wasn't anywhere to be seen. Maybe he was busy with something else. She sent him a quick text.

Hey, Dylan, still up for meeting tonight?

She'd wait a little while, give him more time. She leaned back with her eyes closed and inhaled the warm aroma of woodsmoke from the fireplace.

The next thing she knew, someone's hand shook her shoulder. When she opened her eyes, a stranger's face appeared right in front of her.

"Miss? Are you okay?"

Heat climbed up her neck when she spotted his employee nametag. "I'm sorry, I was waiting for someone." She checked the time on her phone and bit back a gasp. Ten o'clock? "Did anyone else show up?"

The employee shrugged, confusion crossing his face.

Dylan hadn't come all evening? She scanned her phone for missed calls or texts. Nothing.

If she sat here any longer, she'd fall asleep again. She had zero energy to process the fact he hadn't shown up to see her and it would be too late to call. Slipping her arms through her jacket, she made her way back to her room for the night. She'd address the situation tomorrow morning.

———

DYLAN SCRUBBED his face as he sat at the same small table in the lodge's restaurant that he'd occupied for the last several days. He sipped from a mug of hot coffee, then reached for another container of creamer. How many cups of coffee would it take to clear the fog from his brain?

"Dylan?"

He glanced up to find Jocelyn standing in front of him with a plate of food in her hands. Relief and anxiety warred within. Nonetheless, he gestured for her to sit.

She appeared as exhausted as he felt. Surely, she hadn't lain awake half the night because of a nightmare about the past?

"Are you skiing today?"

He scrubbed his face again. "If I can wake up a little more."

She sat but left her food untouched. "Are you okay?"

He shrugged in lieu of an answer.

"You didn't show up last night."

"I'm sorry." He rubbed his face again. He could read the question in her eyes but didn't know how to explain all that had gone through his head since the night before last. The conversation over missions lingered in his mind far into the night after they'd talked. Yesterday, he'd skied with Ethan all day in an effort to ignore the hauntingly similar lifepaths that were laid before him and Jocelyn—hers by choice, and his by God's calling.

I'm not traveling with another loved one into the mission field again. I can't.

He studied her as she picked at her food. Where was the ravenous woman with an enormous appetite and boundless energy? "Are you okay?"

"We had to call in a life-flight medical evac yesterday." She ate a little of her eggs.

He'd heard something about that. Happened sometime midday when he and Ethan were skiing runs on the other side of the mountain. He prayed the kid had received the necessary help and was in recovery now.

"I made that call, and I can't stop wondering if I could've done more."

He listened for the next ten minutes as she recapped the harrowing event.

After she unloaded, her appetite returned. Partially.

"Sounds like you did everything you could." He smiled and drank more coffee.

"Thanks." She expelled a heavy breath. "I know it's true. But sometimes it's hard to feel that way on the inside."

He reached across the table and squeezed her hand. She blinked rapidly for a moment before recovering and continuing her meal.

What would it be like to pursue this thing, whatever was going on between them, after he left tomorrow? He'd warred over it all last evening, concluding that he wasn't ready. But here, now, holding her hand, he couldn't think straight, couldn't pin down why he would've ever made that decision.

She glanced up at him with a sort of reserved hope in her expression. "Will you ski with me today?"

Before he could think better of it, he nodded. "I'd love to."

CHAPTER SEVEN

L ate that afternoon, Jocelyn disembarked from the ski lift and slid to a stop, with Dylan not far behind. Here, halfway up the mountain, she had a bird's eye view of the lower lodge and hotel. A smaller upper lodge and restaurant available to resort skiers only, loomed behind them, promising a rustic and romantic reprieve from the cold. She grinned and cut a glance toward Dylan.

His gentle and handsome smile in return, which he'd held the entire day they'd been skiing together, sent her stomach tumbling yet again. She'd not felt this much exhilaration while being with another man since college.

"I hope that beautiful smile means you're hungry."

Heat infused her cheeks as her stomach grumbled.

"Will you have dinner with me?" He gestured toward the lodge behind them. "I haven't had a chance to try the upper lodge yet. We could take the gondola back down afterward."

She nodded, anticipation swirling inside. "I'd love that."

He grinned, his eyes crinkling with laughter. "I'd like to think it's dinner you're excited about, but I knew you wouldn't say no to a gondola ride."

That he'd recalled her earlier comments about the gondola elicited another grin. "I'd have said yes regardless."

He laughed and bumped her shoulder.

The restaurant here was smaller and more intimate, with small tables bathed in the warm glow of hanging lamps, and spectacular views of the trees and mountain peaks through huge two-story windows. Her stomach fluttered. This was certainly much more than just dinner.

She slipped into the restroom to assess the severity of her appearance. Man, but she was tired from a long week of skiing. Ugh. She could do little to tame her messy and sweaty hair after a full day of skiing, but nonetheless if she were going on a date, she had to try.

She washed her face and combed her fingers through her hair, taming it as best she could.

She emerged from the bathroom and nearly collided with Renee, who still wore her ski patrol jacket and beanie. Renee's eyes widened. "What are you doing up here? I thought you'd have left by now."

Jocelyn opened her mouth, then closed it again.

Renee's eyes widened further. "You're on a date, aren't you?"

Jocelyn pulled Renee into the bathroom and shut the door. "Shh."

"I can't believe it. Well, maybe I can." Renee giggled and tried to poke her head out the door, but Jocelyn dragged her back. "Have you been with him all day?"

"Sometimes I think you're even younger than you say you are."

Renee giggled again. "I wondered what he was doing up here when I saw him standing out there. I have to tell you something. I looked him up online and—"

Jocelyn rolled her eyes. "Please, Renee. I don't have time for gossip. He's waiting on me."

Chatter filled Renee's radio at her hip.

"Looks like you've got to go." She gently shoved Renee out the door. "So say no more about this, and we'll talk when you get back to Trinity Lakes."

"I'm serious. Listen, Jocelyn—"

Jocelyn glared at her. "Is he a convicted felon? On parole? Or being indited for something?"

Renee shook her head.

"Then text me about it later."

Dylan approached both with a smile. "Ready?"

Renee bolted off, apparently forgetting about using the restroom. Dylan only gave her a passing glance before refocusing on Jocelyn. "I put our name in and rented a locker for all our stuff."

"Great."

After they stowed their belongings and skis, they returned to wait for a table. Jocelyn admired the long dark wooden beams across the ceiling as their hostess led them through the dimly lit restaurant. Of course, the server had seated them beside the window overlooking perfect white slopes and rolling hills of pines. A candle flickered in the middle of their table.

Her heart leapt with anticipation as she perused her menu. *Relax, Joss. You've been here before.* But never on a date like this.

Dinner was delicious. While she ate, the fading sunlight turned the tops of the trees and the mountain peak different shades of orange. Then the sun set behind the hills, and the clouds exploded into reds and pinks and purples. Dylan reached for her hand, and she couldn't think of a more perfect night.

How had she fallen this hard this fast?

He paid for dinner—*swoon*—then they gathered their skis and belongings from the lockers and headed over to the gondolas that would take them back across the park to the main lodge and hotel.

Though one gondola was large enough to hold six people, they somehow found themselves alone for the fifteen-minute ride back. Dim overhead lights allowed them to find a seat safely, but otherwise darkness cloaked everything around them.

As they glided through the darkness, Dylan wrapped his arm around her shoulders, then pointed out the huge window. "Look at the lights of Trinity Lakes." She turned and found herself nestled in his arms as she surveyed the beauty of the lights glittering in the distance, spilling horizontally along the far shore of Lake Wainscott. Then above to the northwest, more lights, spread out among the hills, possibly the Bible college and seminary campuses. Maybe the Northshore gated community nestled in between.

"It's beautiful." A picture-perfect sight, if a bit far away.

"I couldn't agree more." Dylan's voice rumbled in her ear, gentle and heady.

She could feel the intensity of his stare and turned to find he wasn't studying the scene out the window. Instead, he focused solely on her. He ran a hand through her hair, twining a bit around his fingers. Her heart hiccupped and she couldn't resist doing the same thing to his hair.

Before they reached the bottom, his mouth met hers in a delicious, incredible kiss that made her grateful she was seated. He broke the kiss and pressed his forehead to hers while he caught his breath.

"I must confess, Jocelyn, I never thought I'd feel this way again."

Pressure built behind her eyes. She hadn't either, not after the nasty breakup she'd had years ago. She'd avoided relation-ships for so long because of it.

But losing a spouse had to be much, much worse than some bad breakup.

When the gondola deposited them at the lower lodge, they disembarked and gathered their skis and poles from the outside container. In a euphoric haze, she floated alongside Dylan through the lodge and back to the hotel.

He insisted on walking her, skis and all, to her room. Once there, she set her skis and poles against the wall, and he did the same. Before she could open her door, he enveloped her again and captured her lips a second time, this one as intense as the first. She held on to his jacket for balance as he ran his fingers through her hair.

"Might want to wait until I wash my hair. I promise it'd be a lot less grimy."

He chuckled and kissed her again, then pressed his forehead to hers. "Will I get that opportunity before you leave?"

Her heart raced as she giggled. It'd been so long since she'd dolled herself up for anyone, let alone a man who'd so quickly stolen her heart.

"When can I see you again?"

"Whenever you want."

"For breakfast?"

She nodded and couldn't resist another kiss.

Finally, he inched backward enough to allow her to turn and unlock her door. Temptation swam in her veins. Her roommates had left yesterday. Nothing and no one would stop her if she invited him inside.

That was the exact mistake she'd made with her ex. They'd both taken things too far too fast—not this fast, though—but she regretted every single moment of that first encounter where she'd allowed him to go too far. It had been their undoing.

Since she'd returned to Trinity Lakes, though she'd been hurt by her mom's abandonment, she recommitted her life to Christ, and pledged to remain steadfast in her relationships with men, which meant waiting until marriage.

She turned to face Dylan again, her heart pounding. If she unlocked that door, that temptation to invite him in could overwhelm her. *God, please give us strength.*

He blinked, concern in his eyes, as if he knew the dilemma swirling within. "Can I bring your skis inside?"

She held a hand to his chest. "Only if you promise not to stay."

He cradled her neck and his eyes shone with compassion as he nodded once. "I promise."

After he left, keeping his promise, she lay in bed wrapped in a wash of gratefulness and affection for this man who seemed too good to be true.

———

DYLAN TORE everything from his luggage bag and emptied it onto his bed, then searched every pocket of every pair of pants. He'd just had his phone this morning while eating breakfast with Jocelyn before they'd all left the resort. Now he couldn't find it anywhere. *Where is it? Where could it possibly be?*

He'd left the resort with it. In fact, he remembered using it in the car while they drove back to Trinity Lakes. How could he have lost the phone in less than an hour and a half?

When he still couldn't find it, he turned the bag upside down and shook it for good measure. Frustration caused him to release a growl.

Ethan emerged from the hall bathroom clothed in a dry hoodie and sweats. "Everything okay?"

He shook his head. The chaotic evidence of his fruitless half-hour search lay at his feet. "I think I might've dropped my phone in one of your bags. Or in the car?"

"Still can't find it?" Ethan walked to his room and returned with his luggage bags. Together they dumped the contents of every bag on top of Dylan's bed and rummaged through every single item. Then they checked every zipped nook and cranny.

Nothing.

He bent his forehead to the bed and growled in frustration.

"Relax, man. Go check the car."

He swiped Ethan's keys from the hook in the kitchen and

spent another half hour scouring every crevasse of Ethan's Trailblazer.

Searching beneath the seats in the far back, his hand finally connected with something cold and flat that felt like a phone. Snatching it up, he expelled a breath of relief, until he noticed a huge crack that spider-webbed outward from the center of the screen like it'd been stepped on. Really?

Maybe the screen would still work enough for him to read his messages. He pressed the power button, but nothing happened. Growling, he shut and locked Ethan's car then stalked into the house.

"Any luck?" Ethan turned from where he stood in the kitchen.

"Phone is busted." He tossed his broken phone on the coffee table and sank to the couch. He curled forward, his hands clasped in front of him. "I didn't save her number anywhere, Ethan. I didn't even write it down."

Ethan leaned against the wall that divided the kitchen from the lounge room, arms crossed, brow furrowed. "I'm sorry, man. That's frustrating."

Frustrating was an understatement. He bent his head, his heart aching. How could he be so careless?

"Does it turn on?" Ethan picked up the phone but discovered the same thing Dylan had. No power. "First, let's plug it in and see if the screen comes on." Ethan found a charger and plugged it in, then turned toward him. "Second, we should pray about it."

He nodded, and Ethan voiced a quick and to the point prayer.

Afterward, Ethan rested a hand on his shoulder for a moment. "It's not the end of the world. You can always order a new phone, right?"

He shook his head. Maybe, yeah. But Jocelyn's number had been in a text message, not saved into his contacts. Why hadn't he made time to do that? What was wrong with him? He'd been out of the dating game way too long.

Devastation broke through him. He had nothing but her first and last name. Why hadn't he found out more about her? Sure, she lived in the same town, but there were nearly ten thousand people in Trinity Lakes, if you counted the population up in the hills and the ranches surrounding the town. And more than that when tourism peaked.

He could call the resort ski patrol office, but her supervisor, though professional, had appeared visibly unhappy with her that first night they'd met. He remembered that much, despite having his head knocked in. The last thing he wanted was for people to think him some kind of stalker.

Maybe he could look her up on a local online residential directory? But that meant he'd need to call every Jocelyn Monroe in town until he found the right one. That seemed creepy and stalkerish too—just one step above walking around town asking if anyone happened to know the beautiful local paramedic.

He wasn't that desperate.

Was he?

Maybe, by some miracle, she attended the same church and he'd see her there. Or he could church hop and try each one. But that would take weeks.

Ethan left Dylan alone and returned to the kitchen.

Fingers crossed, Dylan tried to power on his phone. Nothing but lines of light that flickered on and off. Awesome. Looked like he'd be ordering a new phone for Christmas.

Until then, he'd have to find Jocelyn another way.

CHAPTER EIGHT

Dylan woke up gasping, remnants of the muddy street drenched in rain, and images of a crumpled open-air jeep still lingering like wisps of toxic gas. He scrubbed his face and inhaled deep, slow breaths to calm his accelerated heart rate.

Nearly four in the morning. Awesome. With a six o'clock wake-up call, he wasn't likely to get any more sleep before then.

After a shower, with coffee brewing, Dylan sat in the dim light of the kitchen and ran his hands through his wet hair. He loved teaching only two full days a week, but on days like today, the sharp schedule change wrecked him.

He opened his Bible, but his head still ached from the nightmares. Maybe he should seek out therapy again, as Ethan had suggested. *Lord, I thought I was past all this.* He'd had consistent therapy for over three years already, before moving to the States.

Instead of reading, he bowed his head to pray. *Why are these nightmares coming back, and what would You have me do about it? Can You help me, please?*

No answer.

The relationship he'd begun with Jocelyn must be rekindling all his tucked-away memories of Elise. No, that wasn't completely true. He'd begun having flashbacks when he moved back here in August. Back in her hometown. Wandering the seminary campus they'd attended together.

But Jocelyn …

What must she be thinking now, after two days? That he'd ghosted her, after their beautiful, romantic weekend? He winced at the devastation she must be feeling. Because of his carelessness in not saving, or writing down, her contact information.

At least his phone delivery date had been moved up from Friday to tomorrow. God willing, he'd be able to recover his old information in his new phone. But if her name hadn't been saved in as a contact … would his old texts even show up?

Maybe she'd call him once he got his new phone, and things would miraculously work out.

I know I'm asking a lot, Lord. He huffed out a heavy breath. *I know You can handle it, but I could really use some wisdom when it comes to Jocelyn. Please, don't let her become hurt because of my stupidity.*

He felt more than heard one word impressed upon his heart. **Wait.**

The same word he'd felt all week. Just one word. No other explanation.

He shook his head and scrubbed his eyes again. Lot of good that shower did, as fog still encased his brain.

Wait for what, Lord?

He'd already spent so many years stuck in quicksand, waiting for what, he didn't know.

Then, when Ethan suggested he come to Trinity Lakes for an extended visit, maybe work here at the college for a bit, he'd been amazed at how quickly all the pieces had fallen into place.

For the first time in years, he'd stepped out of the mire and onto solid ground.

Now, he'd found a woman he thought he could fall in love with, someone who inspired him to push forward in life again. And God was telling him to wait. Made absolutely no sense.

He shook his head and turned his attention to class prep.

A cold December wind blew down from the mountains, and a light dusting of snow covered the ground outside. Dylan rode with Ethan the short mile drive toward the seminary campus, which faced the north side of Lake Wainscott. He usually enjoyed a peaceful walk through the campus grounds that could be accessed through the back of their gated townhouse community. Pines and oaks mingled together, littering the ground with needles, and yellow and golden leaves. But with the temperature below freezing outside, he opted for a ride where heat blasted against him.

Ethan cast a side glance toward him as they entered the car park. "You look exhausted. What time did you wake up? I thought I heard the shower in the middle of the night."

Dylan frowned and remained silent. Just like Elise, Ethan loved to rise with the dawn. Dylan, however, would rather stay up with the moon. How did people function when they woke up with the sun?

The familiar pang of loneliness rolled over him. Elise would go for a morning run, returning home to find him still asleep. She'd often crawl back in bed to wake him up, still wearing her tracksuit.

Ethan parked and gathered his briefcase. Then he shot a look at Dylan, like something shocking had come to mind. "I have an idea. What if she left you a voicemail? You could get check your voicemails on my phone and get her number that way."

Hope ignited in his chest as he gathered his briefcase and laptop bag. "Worth a shot."

While they walked together, Dylan dialed his phone number, then with the press of a few buttons, found his voicemails and listened to one from Mum. No voicemails popped up from Jocelyn.

He handed the phone back. "She hasn't left me a message." Why did disappointment sink like a rock in his stomach?

"Come by during lunch. If she's as interested in you as you are in her, she'll eventually leave a voicemail."

Dylan agreed, and they parted ways.

After his first class, Dylan gathered up the materials he'd brought and headed out the door, sufficiently distracted from thoughts of the dark morning hours.

In the hall, he spotted a familiar face, smiling, and child-like. Could it be that young ski patroller who had first arrived to check on him after he and the snowboarder had collided? What was her name again? Renee?

It couldn't be. Could it really? He paused, hesitant. Wait. Weren't all those nearby her students of his? No, that was ridiculous. It would be too much of a coincidence.

Renee turned from her friends, caught his eye, and smiled again. Leaving her group, she approached him. "Hey, Dr. Mackay."

"Renee, isn't it? From the resort ski patrol?"

She nodded once. "That's right."

"Have you been in my class this entire semester?"

She smiled, nodding. "But not this one. I'm in your evening class. I have friends in this one."

"You didn't recognize me on the mountain?"

She shook her head. "You didn't recognize me, either."

"Well, I suppose we were both all decked out in snow gear from head to toe." He quirked up one side of his mouth. "I've also seen over a hundred different students this semester."

She nodded and blinked. "Have you talked to Jocelyn?"

"My phone broke on Sunday. I've ordered another one. Should be here tomorrow." His heart hiccupped. Maybe she could relay the info so that Jocelyn didn't think he'd ghosted her. "Do you see her often?"

Renee hugged a laptop case to her chest. "She's a student here as well, so our paths cross when she's not working."

She was a student? Here? No, no, no, no, no. His heart caved in, crashing so hard he reached for the nearby wall with his free hand to steady himself.

"Ah … if you see her, please pass on the message that I've ordered a new phone." He stepped backward. "And I'm sorry—." He clamped his mouth shut. Already bad enough that Renee knew about them being together. If even one staff member knew they were going out together, then word could get round to campus admin and he would be in hot water before the day's end.

This was really, truly bad. He'd assumed she'd been doing her nursing degree online or somewhere else nearby. He hadn't even known they offered nursing here. Must've been added during all the years he'd been overseas.

Why hadn't he found out more about her before they'd left the resort? His impulsive decisions and carelessness would not only cost him the woman of his dreams, they could cost him his job and only income.

Renee stood waiting for him to finish his sentence.

He inhaled a shaky breath. Though risky, he had to talk to Jocelyn again. He couldn't pretend nothing had happened between them. Then he really would be ghosting her, and he didn't want to hurt her like that. "When is she on campus?"

"Monday, Wednesday, and Friday."

He nodded once. "Thank you." He turned, ignoring the guilt that he'd run off so abruptly. Explaining himself would only put himself and Jocelyn in jeopardy.

What am I going to do?

———

JOCELYN LAY across the couch in her living room, exhausted, her mind spinning. Three days and he hadn't called, texted, or replied to any of her calls. But they'd been texting all weekend, so he had her number, right?

Now, every time she called, his phone went to voicemail. Obviously, he hadn't been receiving her texts. She'd finally left him a voicemail earlier today during lunch. But he hadn't returned that either.

Tears burned her eyes. Three days. *Three. Days.* Why wasn't he calling her back? All the drama made doing the mountain of homework she had twice as difficult. *This is ridiculous. I'm being ridiculous.*

Had all of it been a ruse? Some kind of scam? She had no idea where he and Ethan lived—did they even live in Trinity Lakes?—or where they worked. Why hadn't she asked more questions?

Had he suddenly decided that dating again was too hard? Why would he ignore her like this?

Jesse's words about the possibility of him lying to her floated through her mind. Could he have made up the whole story about not being married? Maybe he was actually separated, and they'd gotten back together once he'd returned home? She blinked back hot, angry tears. *Why is dating so incredibly hard?*

Her phone vibrated and Renee's face popped up on the screen. Not tonight. She couldn't deal with a conversation right now. Exhaustion tugged her down against the couch. Emergency calls came nonstop today, and taken them all over the county, and up into the sticks. That, coupled with having to ride with an inexperienced new driver who kept her adrenaline pumping even while dispatch was silent, left her wanting to curl up in bed right now.

Renee called again. She flipped the phone over and focused on her TV screen.

This time, her phone pinged a different sound. Renee left a text message. Fine, she could read a text.

What was this? Why would Renee send her a link to the seminary website?

She clicked on it and when it uploaded, a handsome and professional headshot of Dylan appeared, along with an employee biography beneath. He was a Biblical Theology professor? At the same school where she attended?

No. Way.

She scrambled up and called Renee back.

"He teaches at the seminary?" she said before Renee could even say hello.

"He teaches one of my evening classes."

"Are you absolutely sure?"

"Dr. Dylan Mackay, right? Did you check the link I sent? He's got that same swoony Australian accent and everything. I think he teaches at the seminary on Tuesdays and Thursdays. And sometimes he lectures at the Bible college too. I asked around."

Jocelyn rubbed her forehead, both baffled and relieved. Then she closed her eyes against another wave of emotion. Her classes were Monday, Wednesday, Friday—she worked twelve-hour shifts on Tuesday and Thursday. After graduation at the end of December, she'd be back to working four days on, three days off again.

Not really missing that now.

"He said his phone broke and that he'd ordered a new phone."

"You talked to him?" Hope filled Jocelyn's chest, pressing against her heart like a physical force. Maybe he'd been telling the truth all along. "That explains everything." She covered her mouth. No wonder she couldn't contact him. "Thanks for letting me know, Renee. I appreciate it."

After she hung up, she read and reread his bio. Relief washed through her. Much of what was written matched the small snippets he'd revealed to her—except the death of his wife. But she'd not expect something that morbid to be included in a professional biography.

Hope renewed, she flipped off the lights and lay in bed watching a movie on her laptop. He'd call her again, right? Eventually. And they'd run into each other again. They had to, even if she had to orchestrate it. This blossoming, more-than-friends relationship was not over, not if she had anything to say about it.

She closed her eyes to pray.

The Bible says You care about every matter of our heart. Can You please help me figure this thing out between us? It's been killing me inside. Even with this new revelation, everything is so up in the air. Please, Lord, I need your help.

CHAPTER NINE

Dylan lounged on the couch with the TV on, completely oblivious to what channel he'd switched to.

Ethan entered and hung his coat in a small closet near the doorway, then laid his briefcase and laptop bag on a kitchen chair. He stopped to stare at Dylan. "Everything okay? I didn't catch you at lunch."

Dylan curled forward and scrubbed his face. "Jocelyn is a student at the seminary."

Ethan sucked in an audible breath, frozen in place. "You found her? How …?" He rubbed his clean-shaven chin. "She never said anything while you were skiing together?"

He shook his head. "She mentioned she was studying nursing. It never even crossed my mind that we had a nursing program …" He rubbed his forehead. This wasn't her fault. "I'm the one who never said anything about where I worked. Had I mentioned something, this whole thing could've been avoided."

Ethan whistled. "Did you talk to her yet? How did you find out?"

Dylan leaned back against the couch and closed his eyes. "I haven't seen her. I ran into a friend of hers who told me she attended the seminary. Of course, she attends on the days I'm not teaching."

Ethan perched himself on the edge of an armchair. "Are you going to break things off?"

Dylan raised his gaze to Ethan's. "Of course. I have to. Or risk losing my job." He prayed it wasn't already too late and that gossip hadn't spread. In this small town, gossip could spread like a bushfire.

"Oh. A package came. Might be for you." Ethan walked outside, then returned with a small rectangular package with his phone company logo on it.

The irony of the situation hit like a fist to his stomach. Getting the phone any earlier wouldn't have helped, as he wouldn't have been able to recover his text messages anyway.

Ethan leaned against the wall that divided the kitchen from the lounge room, one ankle crossed over the other. "I'm really sorry, Dylan."

Dylan thanked Ethan, took his package, and retreated to his room. He tossed it on his bed, then showered. It was what it was. He'd made the right call. He wasn't going to quit his job for a woman he'd known for less than two weeks, no matter how perfect she might be.

FRIDAY MORNING, Jocelyn bolted from her first class as soon as the professor dismissed them.

She hadn't seen or heard from Dylan since Sunday. Her nerves danced every time she navigated through the pathways throughout campus. Where could he be? Why hadn't he called her yet? Shouldn't he have gotten a replacement phone by now? She'd texted him and left a voicemail at least once a day after her conversation with Renee on Tuesday night, but she didn't want to seem as totally desperate as she felt, so she'd eased up.

Rounding a corner, she collided with Renee.

Renee grabbed her shoulders. "Have you seen or heard from him?"

Jocelyn shook her head. "Not yet."

They fell in step together and navigated toward Renee's next class. Jocelyn's stomach rumbled with nerves and anxiousness. "Do you think he'll call me again? It's been three whole days. Six since he broke his phone. What if he's not telling the truth?"

"You said yourself that he didn't seem like the lying type."

"Yes, but why didn't he tell me he was teaching here?" She expelled a heavy breath, trying to contain the whirlwind of feelings she held for Dylan. Unwillingly, her mind tracked back to her last relationship. Mick had been charming, sucking her in with gifts and overt displays of affection, and convincing her to sleep with him. All that affection had gradually dissipated—then she discovered he'd been cheating on her.

"Dr. Mackay seems really nice. If he's teaching here, he's definitely a believer, so I think it's safe to say you can ask him what's going on and he'll be honest with you."

Jocelyn frowned and mulled over the logic in Renee's words. He must be a Christian to be teaching biblical theology, of all things. But even Christian professors were only human, and humans lied and cheated.

A thought sideswiped her, like a gut punch, stopping her in her tracks. Would they even be able to continue a relationship if she were a student? Maybe if she weren't in any of his classes.

This relationship may have been doomed before it began.

Renee stopped alongside her. "You okay?"

Jocelyn inhaled a breath, forced a smile and a single nod. She glanced toward the two-story library to their left. The sun glinted off the two-story-tall windows. "I'll head to the library after class. Meet you there later?" Renee nodded, they hugged, and before parting ways, Jocelyn promised to keep her updated.

During her class, she flipped through the selfies she and

Dylan had taken while skiing and snowmobiling. She should have taken a photo on the gondola, but it'd been too dark.

Just the thought of their kiss that night sent her heart racing again, in spite of the doom that hung over her fragile hope, an imminent rainstorm that threatened to burst at any second. Regardless, they had to talk again.

Without a clue as to how he would find her, she could do nothing but follow her normal routine. On such a small campus, she had to run into him sometime.

The dusting of snow from yesterday still covered the ground in a thin, frosty white blanket. Spindly tree branches reached for the sky as she navigated toward the campus library. Evergreen pines and spruces stood tall in the distance, surrounding most of the campus. The grounds positioned on a rise afforded the students beautiful views of Lake Wainscott, and the river flowing into it from the northern mountain range.

She rounded a corner, then paused as her stomach flipped with anticipation. Dylan sat on a bench, a forest green scarf round his neck. He looked dignified and professional in a thick peacoat and brown slacks. Seeing him in this element, outside of his ski garb was … thrilling.

His briefcase sat beside him, and he was bent over, concentrating on a stack of papers. The brown hair he wore so well curled at his forehead. How long had he waited out here in the cold for her to pass by him?

"Dylan?"

He glanced up, but where she expected to see a handsome smile, she saw a furrowed brow and downturned mouth. Not good signs. Her stomach churned.

He gestured for her to sit. She stashed her stuff beside the bench, but when she leaned toward him for a hug, he held up a hand.

Wait, what?

She forged ahead regardless. "It's so good to see you again. I talked to Renee. I'm sorry to hear about your phone. I tried calling and texting in case you hadn't saved my number."

He nodded and rubbed his forehead, then eyed her directly. "You're a student here?"

She nodded.

"Why didn't you tell me?"

Defensiveness rose inside. "It's not like you were forthcoming with me. You didn't tell me you were a professor. I at least mentioned I was a student finishing my degree."

"Yes, but I assumed you were part of an online nursing program because ..." He inhaled abruptly, cutting off whatever last words he'd planned to say. His eyes swirled with sadness. "Jocelyn... I cannot date students."

She sucked in a breath as she sat back.

"It's not just frowned upon. It's against the rules, and I could be terminated." He gathered his papers and placed them into his briefcase. "I don't want you to get into any trouble. For your safety, as well as mine, you should stop calling."

Her heart caved in on itself. He wanted to completely cut ties?

"I apologize. All of the blame rests on me for rushing into things and not being as forthcoming as I should've been."

"Dylan."

He held up a hand again and implored her with his eyes to let it rest. Emotion rose in her throat, but she willed it back down. "It wasn't just you, though." Still, her voice wavered.

He stood, and she stood with him.

"Then I think maybe both of us would do well to learn from this."

Unable to refute his statement, she watched him turn and walk away, and struggled to keep her tears at bay.

CHAPTER TEN

Saturday, Dylan slept until noon and woke to find the house empty. At least he'd slept through the night. Spending the week trying to forget about Jocelyn while still performing all his work responsibilities had left him exhausted.

He forced himself out of bed, ate breakfast for lunch, then spent the rest of the day catching up on grading.

He found a local college football game to watch on TV. Nothing like rugby league or Aussie rules football, but it would do as white noise. After hours of grading all the backlog of essays that had accumulated before Thanksgiving, while attempting to fill the silence with football—anything to drown out his dreary thoughts—his brain was fried hotter than a fresh meat patty.

His phone pinged with a text from Ethan.

Staying at Lillian's for dinner tonight. Want to catch lunch together tomorrow?

Dylan leaned his head back against the couch and closed his eyes. Just as well. He'd not want to be around himself tonight, given the choice.

Sunday, Dylan woke to pounding on his bedroom door. "Dylan, wake up."

Ethan. What in the world did he want? Dylan rolled away, putting his back to the door.

Of course, Ethan proceeded to make as much noise as possible in the kitchen. Dylan pulled the pillow over his ears. Ear plugs were next on his shopping list if this was to become a regular thing.

Sometime later, Ethan opened Dylan's door without permission. "Come on. We've got church."

Dylan rolled back over and pulled the blankets higher over his head.

Ethan whistled from the hall bathroom, the tune competing with the sound of his electric razor. "Come on. You don't ever miss church."

Dylan growled. "I'm warning Lillian about your morning antics."

A laugh filled the hallway, spilling into Dylan's open door. "I'll be sure to warn her that you're warning her."

Now fully awake, he wouldn't get back to sleep even if Ethan left him here. Being alone yesterday had been misery. Maybe going to church would be good for him. As far as he knew, Jocelyn didn't attend the same church. There were multiple churches scattered throughout Trinity Lakes. Outside of that, she likely ran in different friendship circles than him, with other young adults her own age.

To his credit, Ethan ignored Dylan's downcast mood, acting as if nothing were amiss.

At the end of service, he, Ethan, and Lillian walked together out into the foyer. Lillian excused herself for a moment to speak with a friend, and Ethan promised to wait.

Ethan snagged a cup off the small coffee bar and filled it with the hot brew. "Come to lunch with us?"

Dylan frowned. Being the third wheel was not his idea of a

relaxing Sunday afternoon. "Think I'll take a raincheck on that." He could catch an NFL game instead, and grade in peace and quiet ... while trying in vain to rid his mind of Jocelyn.

Ethan's easy smile faded as he lifted the cup to drink. He inclined his head toward the far corner of the foyer. "Dr. Graham is headed this way."

Dylan's stomach sank, though he'd been half-dreading some kind of call or email all week long. He couldn't decide which was worse, discussing his situation in Dr. Graham's office, or in the middle of a church crowd.

Dr. Graham approached with a cordial smile and offered his greetings. After shaking each of their hands, his smile waned as he eyed Dylan directly. "I wondered if you had a moment to talk?"

Dylan nodded once, and he and Ethan allowed the older gentleman to usher them into a more private alcove.

Ethan stood tall, shoulders back, with a familiar stance of defensiveness in his demeanor that Dylan recognized from years gone by. "What's this about?"

The president sipped from a foam cup of coffee, exchanged a glance with Ethan, then leveled another serious gaze on Dylan. "I have been hearing rumors that you're dating a student who attends the seminary."

Dylan's throat went as dry as the outback. He cleared it, wishing for a cup of water from the table across the way. Still, he couldn't answer.

"Where did you hear said rumors?" Ethan asked amid his silence.

"Over Thanksgiving break, another staff member spotted you two having dinner together at a restaurant up at the ski resort." He pinned Dylan with a pointed look. "Is this true?"

Dylan rubbed his eyes and expelled a breath. "I have nothing to hide from you, sir. Yes, I had dinner with a woman who I later discovered was a student. Yes, I am clearly aware of the rules. At the time, I had absolutely no idea she attended the seminary. If I'd known, I'd never have entertained the idea of pursuing her. I've already cleared this matter and haven't contacted her since that conversation."

Dr. Graham folded his arms. "You've never seen her before on campus?"

He shook his head and clamped his mouth shut. Discussing the fact that he knew her work schedule wouldn't do him any favors.

The president glanced at Ethan. "Have you seen her before?"

Ethan folded his arms and shook his head.

The president's brow furrowed. "Does she go to church here?"

Both Ethan and Dylan shook their heads. "We've not seen her," Ethan said.

"As I said, I have nothing to hide." Dylan straightened his stance. "I'd never met or seen her before we met at the resort."

The president mulled over their explanation in silence. Dylan's heart hammered. A glance at Ethan showed his expression remained firm and determined.

How could this have happened? Where was his head? He'd risked his livelihood with his hesitancy to open up amid an imprudent pursuit of a woman he barely knew. He exhaled a slow breath and closed his eyes.

Lord, I need this job. And so does Ethan. Please forgive me for my careless behavior and protect us through this situation.

Dr. Graham drank the rest of his coffee before speaking again. "All right then. I strongly recommend no communication with this woman until she graduates. Whenever that may be."

Dylan nodded without hesitation.

After their conversation ended, Dylan hastily navigated into the car park without waiting for Ethan.

Ethan jogged up behind him. "Hey, Dylan, wait."

"I'm sorry for dragging you into this." He shoved his hands

in his pockets and faced the lake that shone beneath a sky smattered with clouds.

"What are you apologizing for?"

He shook his head and turned to face Ethan. "I was rash and careless, rushing into things with Jocelyn. If I had taken the time to truly get to know her, and to tell her more about myself, none of this would've happened and I wouldn't have put both yours and my job on the line like that." He huffed out a hard breath into the chilly air. "And what if this affects Jocelyn? What if the president goes to speak with her as well?"

"He'd have to know which student she was first." Ethan produced a beanie from his pocket and pulled it over his head. "Will you stop beating yourself up? Mistakes happen. If he talks with her, he'll hear the same story. Right?"

Dylan expelled another breath. What if she told a different story? What if she blamed him for omitting something as commonplace as his career?

"Plus, didn't you say she was close to graduating?"

Dylan lifted a shoulder as he sifted through the conversations they'd had together in November. "Close" could mean she was slated to graduate in May, or in December. He couldn't recall which she'd said.

"Dylan, she really is a wonderful woman. And you had a wonderful time together. Don't discount that. If this girl is the one for you, she'll understand and wait for you, and you can wait on her."

Dylan inhaled more cold air into his lungs. He turned toward the lake. "Think I'll take a walk. Would you mind picking me up later?"

"Is your phone on?"

Dylan paused and held his phone up in the air.

Ethan nodded once. "Text me and I'll pick you up."

Coat zipped to his chin and hands deep in his pockets, Dylan walked the footpaths along the shores of the lake toward the great stone bridge.

Every time he blinked, Jocelyn's smiling face flickered behind his eyes. He missed her with a fierceness he'd not felt since he'd been dating Elise. *This woman ...*

How could he not beat himself up over all this?

He tilted his face toward Heaven and closed his eyes. *Why didn't You tell me to wait before, while we were skiing together? Why did You tell me to wait after the fact?*

Hmm. Seemed he'd been lamenting to God a whole lot as of late. Instead of truly listening, like he should've done over Thanksgiving. Maybe if he'd been listening, he'd have heard God tell him to wait.

In fact, as he contemplated that, he'd been lamenting to God a whole lot over the last several years, more than he had been listening. But the pain had been so difficult. And this new, self-inflicted pain only made matters worse.

Yet, God had remained steadfast, seeing him through. He'd never failed. Never forsaken him. In truth, God had blessed him through his rough-trodden journey of grief. He'd provided for him in the form of a loving and supportive family back in Sydney, who'd encouraged him to seek therapy and pulled him back to his feet. And He provided for him now in the form of a place to live, a steadfast friendship, and a career where he could teach others about God's word.

And, if the conversation with Dr. Graham were any indication, he'd granted Dylan grace and another chance to make things right. As He always did.

Lord, thank You for sparing myself and Ethan thus far. Thank You for allowing us to continue to provide for ourselves and to continue to teach Your Word.

Thank You, Lord, for my family, for their stalwart support, their love and encouragement, and willingness to help me get back on my feet. Thank You for Ethan, for his steadfast friendship through the most challenging time in my life. Thank You for his wisdom and calm nature, and his cheerful demeanor.

And thank You for Jocelyn. For the beautiful soul that she is. Lord, whatever You have planned for each of us individually, guide my steps and guide hers.

He inhaled the scent of water and earth and pine. Though a measure of peace washed through him, his heart still ached, still longed to be with Jocelyn. If they had their second chance, whenever that may be, he wouldn't rush this time. He wouldn't make the same careless mistakes as before.

CHAPTER ELEVEN

The next week dragged by. Dylan kept to himself in the evenings after work, while Ethan spent time with Lillian. Dylan didn't blame the guy one bit. The Christmas season always began early in Trinity Lakes, and all the decorations and festivities downtown tended to bring out the opportunity for romance in a relationship. Dylan was happy for Ethan. Truly.

If only he could share this season with Jocelyn. If only he knew when she was supposed to graduate. But he couldn't seek her out, and he dared not talk to her friend either.

At least he'd caught up on grading.

One Saturday evening in early December, Ethan arrived home, a smile on his face as usual. He stopped and surveyed the papers Dylan had stacked in assorted piles across the coffee table.

Ethan frowned at him. Dylan folded his arms and returned the frown. What? This was how he graded. This or at the kitchen table.

"A bunch of us are getting together at Joe's Diner tonight. Want to join?"

"Not tonight, mate."

Ethan laid his coat over the arm of the couch. "Come on, man, you've been a hermit all week. No more moping."

"I'm not moping." Really, he'd tried to seek God's peace regularly.

"She's not dead, you know."

Dylan scowled. How could he say that? "No, she's just totally unavailable, which is almost worse."

"What are you, twenty?" Laughter lit Ethan's eyes. "Come on. Going out will do you good."

"For your information, I haven't been moping." Dylan gestured to the piles of papers. "I've been grading."

"In sweats. All day." Ethan grinned.

Dylan sat back again and scrubbed his beard. Where Ethan assumed laziness or moping, Dylan preferred to define it as the beauty of working from home three days a week.

"You've got half an hour to get dressed and put your stuff away." Ethan disappeared into his room, leaving Dylan alone.

What was wrong with sitting at home? He was just fine right here. Away from people. Anger simmered in his gut.

When Ethan returned from his room, Dylan stood and glared at him. "I don't appreciate coming all the way to the States to hear the same line from my brother-in-law that I heard from my family."

Ethan eyed him. "Then maybe there's something to it, if I'm saying the same thing as they are."

Forty minutes later, Dylan found himself walking behind Ethan into Joe's Diner, one of the more casual eateries in Trinity Lakes. He and Ethan had eaten here a handful of times before. Now, a red and green Christmas wreath hung in the doorway and small lit Christmas trees and greenery covered every open counter. Twinkling lights were strung up along the back wall.

In the back corner of the packed diner sat a loud group, some of them clad in blue uniformed shirts with EMERGENCY stamped on the back.

Jocelyn sat among them, laughing, her smile as bright as he remembered.

"Hey."

Ethan's voice jolted Dylan from his trance. He turned back toward the exit, but Ethan grabbed his arm and tugged him back.

"You're awfully skittish for a missionary who traveled into remote villages in Africa."

Dylan scowled at Ethan, but Ethan would not loosen his grip.

"We're sitting on the opposite side of the restaurant." He pointed to a small group of professors seated together in a rounded corner booth, including some familiar faces.

Dylan relented and followed, then sat on the end next to Ethan. He offered obligatory handshakes and waves as Ethan reintroduced him.

From where they sat, he had direct line of sight to Jocelyn, though he doubted she noticed him, given the rowdiness of the group surrounding her. After he ordered, he sat in silence, listening and observing.

He'd downed two glasses of water by the time their food arrived, and in all the waiting he could do nothing but watch Jocelyn as she talked and laughed and joked around. His stomach soured as multiple guys at the table teased and flirted with her. Maybe that was the nature of their job. Didn't matter. The situation irked him, even though he had zero claim on her. His heart ached all over again.

Somehow, Jocelyn noticed him at last, and paused in her conversation. Where he expected to see a smile, or some evidence of excitement, some acknowledgement that she missed him as fiercely as he missed her, he found instead a fixed frown.

Ethan, ever the master of conversation, kept their table engaged in lively discussions over politics and religion, neither of which Dylan cared to contribute to. He hadn't been in

America for several years. While a good biblical theology debate sounded tempting, he nonetheless ate in silence.

At some point, Jocelyn pulled out her phone, typed into it, then set it beside her. Moments later, his phone vibrated in his pocket. He fished it out and read a text.

I graduate at the end of this semester.

He reread the text three times, hope flickering to life with those eight little words.

Another text appeared.

Only three weeks away.

He smiled, unbidden joy struggling to break through the melancholy. As if he didn't know when the semester ended. But would seeking her out right away be appropriate?

He began a text, hesitated, then deleted his intended words. Dr. Graham's warning still hung ever present in the back of his mind. Best to have zero interaction whatsoever.

His finger hovered over the delete option to completely erase the text, but again he hesitated.

Ethan elbowed him in the side then bent down to whisper in his ear. "Are you finally done staring at her now?"

Had he been so obvious? He frowned at Ethan, shoved his phone away and tried his best to focus on the conversation around him for the rest of the meal.

———

JOCELYN PULLED up through the line of cars crawling along the curb at Spokane International Airport and waited behind a pickup truck. A succession of texts came through on her phone from her brother.

Picked up my bags. Heading outside.

I'm here. She sent him a photo of her car she'd taken this morning.

You're still driving that old thing?

Snarky as always. This car had gotten her to and from California just fine, thank you very much. *Well, you could've rented a car instead. Or ordered a rideshare.*

Thanks for saving me a little money.

Much better. She sent him a smiley, then leaned against her car to wait.

When he approached, he wrapped her in a bear hug, lifting her off the ground. "Good to see you, little Joss."

Laughing, she shoved her palms against his chest until he put her down. "You might be taller, but I'm still older."

He laughed, then stowed his bags in her trunk before climbing into the front seat.

On the drive back, Christian music played from the radio. He fiddled with the dial, channel surfing until he found some classic rock station. She shelved her annoyance, choosing instead to be grateful Jake had decided to stay for the next two weeks when she hadn't seen him in person for years.

She cut a glance sideways. His shoulders drooped and the bags under his eyes told her he hadn't slept much lately.

"Everything go all right on the flight over?"

"Yeah." He exhaled and reclined his seat.

"I'm so happy you came to visit."

"Couldn't miss you graduating. Again."

"Look who's talking. You've got two degrees, too."

He shrugged. "Yeah, but I haven't done anything with the business degree yet."

"Don't worry, someday an opportunity will come. It hasn't been that long since you graduated." She flashed a smile at him. "I'm just so glad you're visiting town again. When's the last time you were in Trinity Lakes?"

"Dad's funeral."

That tanked the mood. She frowned and continued driving as rainfall splattered against the windshield.

"So how do you feel? Now that you're about to graduate

again?" His question broke the tense silence that had descended. She exhaled and gripped the wheel with both hands. "Overwhelmed with all the decisions in front of me. Anxious about the nursing exam I have to take. And about going back to work full time."

"Means more money, right?" He threw one arm behind his head and leaned the chair back even farther. "Once you're a legit registered nurse, that'll mean a higher income."

"Yeah, but until then, I could definitely use a roommate." Since her previous roommate had moved out earlier than expected, she'd had to cut into her savings for the last month and a half just to get by.

Rain drummed harder against the windshield. She stopped talking to focus on driving. If it continued, they could run into snow once she reached the higher elevations in Trinity Lakes.

He reclined his head back and interlaced his fingers. In less than five minutes, a soft, familiar snore caught her attention and out of the corner of her eye she could see his eyes were closed.

She spent the rest of the drive stuck in thick traffic, making a two-and-a-half-hour trip take at least an hour longer. All the while, the unknowns sat like rocks in her stomach.

She glanced at Jake's sleeping form again. Would he ever consider moving back? She'd have less financial strain, he'd be close by, and she wouldn't have to consider moving out of Trinity Lakes for a nursing job. Win, win, win. Though she doubted he'd see it the same way. She didn't know the whole story, but Dad said he left Trinity Lakes in a rush sometime after he'd turned twenty. Something about a girl.

On top of everything else, there was Dylan, who still ignored her texts, sparing though they were. What if he had deleted them? What if he didn't plan to contact her at all after she graduated?

It still irked that he hadn't told her anything about where he worked. He hadn't lied, but he still should've said something. But she should've asked. Now she couldn't even go to anyone at the seminary to ask about the specifics of the rules without risking her own future. What if the seminary discouraged staff from dating former students?

The more she contemplated the circumstances of their meeting over Thanksgiving, the more she recognized that just maybe, God had been looking out for them, painful as it was to endure. If Dylan had discovered earlier that she attended the seminary, their friendship would've ended before it even began. And she'd never have gotten to know such a fascinating man. As much as it ached to be ignored by him right now, she understood.

She just wanted to be friends again, but given how strongly she felt, "just friends" didn't seem possible.

Maybe I just need to focus on the now and stop dwelling on things I can't control.

Her brother was here through Christmas! For the first time since Dad's death, she would actually get to physically hang out with him. She couldn't wait to spend time together,

This weekend her coworker had an annual Christmas party planned, and after graduation, she had the Trinity Lakes' annual Christmas Eve parade downtown, and her church's annual Christmas Eve candlelight service to look forward to. 4011`

Businesses and homes all over town were already decked out in festive holiday decorations. White lights strung across downtown streets, homes throughout the neighborhoods covered in colorful lights and Christmas displays, and holly leaves and wreaths hung on every door and lamppost. And, with the way it'd been snowing lately, they'd have snow on Christmas Day. She and the whole town couldn't wait for a white Christmas.

But first, she had to get through graduation.

CHAPTER TWELVE

Dylan followed Ethan as he strode across the central lawn of the seminary campus toward the auditorium where they held graduation ceremonies twice a year. Though a cold wind blew, the sun shone bright and cheerful, and a strong scent of winter hung heavy in the air. White snowfall from the night before coated the ground.

Excited conversation rose from the crowd of family and friends who streamed in ahead and behind them, igniting similar memories of his own graduation years ago. That same exhilaration he'd felt wafted tangibly through the air, along with an uplifting sense of relief and pride.

He blinked against the memory of Elise's bright and joyous smile, and of her family's loving presence surrounding him that day.

He'd not intended to dwell on Elise today, but her memory came stomping into his mind to demand attention whenever it wanted, regardless of his desire. In spite of the ache, he smiled. The insistence of her memories reminded him of her feistiness all the more.

Inside the auditorium, Dylan sat with Ethan and the other

faculty and staff to the right of the graduates. He couldn't resist searching the rows of graduates for Jocelyn's face, but with so many black gowns and caps, it was difficult to decipher which one was Jocelyn.

Until a woman three rows from the front turned her face briefly, her long blonde hair flowing down her back.

Jocelyn. Looking beautiful, with bright eyes, rosy cheeks, and dusky pink lips. His traitorous heart couldn't slow now that he'd spotted her. How long had it been since he'd seen her at the restaurant?

After all the speeches, as the graduates walked across the stage when their names were called, his heart swelled with pride and appreciation, not just for Jocelyn, but for all the graduates.

He knew the intensive work involved in getting both degrees. Completion was a great accomplishment, and every student should feel proud.

Afterward, everyone followed the rows of graduates and filed toward the adjoining ballroom. Dylan followed Ethan as they navigated their way through the crowd.

"The bible college invited me to their annual Christmas dinner," Ethan said. "Want to come along?"

Dylan frowned. "Why not take Lillian?"

"She's not available that night, if you can believe it."

"I'll think about it."

Ethan cut a sideways glance to Dylan as they continued walking. "Are you going to ask her out?"

Dylan shot him a glare. "Come again?"

Ethan did that thing again with his eyebrows, waggling them up and down. "She's officially no longer a student." He used finger quotes to accentuate "officially."

How could Ethan say something like that after their conversation with Dr. Graham? Dylan rubbed his eyes. The last thing he wanted to do was think past today.

As usual, Ethan was all smiles as they entered the large open room, which had been converted into a dining hall of sorts and decorated with gold and silver balloons and bows. Along the wall, round tables draped in white linen cloth were filled with snacks, desserts, and drinks.

A second round of cheers and applause for the graduates rose as they stood in front of the half-filled ballroom.

After the applause died down, Ethan shoved Dylan's shoulder. "Go find her."

"Are you crazy?" Dylan shook his head. He would be treading on thin ice even entertaining the idea of associating with a student in such a manner, official graduate or not.

He surveyed the room where graduates and families mingled together, laughing, and celebrating, and blinked through all the memories again of when he'd gotten his doctorate and Elise had gotten her master's.

He turned toward Ethan and gestured around. "All of this doesn't remind you of Elise?"

"Of course it does." Ethan's smile dimmed, but he still held an air of nonchalance. "If you're asking whether it bothers me, it doesn't." He shrugged one shoulder and moved up in the line toward the buffet. "I think it helps me feel closer to her, because I know she loved it here."

Dylan filled a plate with fruit and moved off to the side. Carrying his own plate of snacks, Ethan cast him one more look before mouthing, "talk to her," and disappearing off into the crowd, no doubt in search of Lillian.

Great. Dylan should be used to this by now. The mate who dragged him places had a habit of disappearing and leaving him to fend for himself.

He ate his fruit and people-watched, unintentionally searching for Jocelyn's face in the crowd. *Stop it.* He couldn't talk to her. No way. That would only encourage the earlier rumors and set both him and her up for trouble.

"Dr. Mackay."

He turned around to find Jocelyn standing behind him, dressed in the prestigious black cap and gown. A fierce inward tug begged him to pull her into his arms and congratulate her properly. Instead, he shoved his free hand into his pocket and smiled politely. But oh, if his heart weren't a throbbing drum inside his chest at the sight of her.

"Congratulations, Ms. Monroe."

"Thanks." She held a plate in one hand, and her degree in the other, as if waiting for him to continue speaking.

He turned behind him, to the table lined with drinks. "Would you like a drink?"

She nodded with that shy smile he'd come to recognize in November. He set his plate aside, filled two glasses with sparkling apple juice and handed one to her.

She tucked her degree beneath her arm and accepted the glass he offered. Once she held it steady, he tapped his glass against hers. "Another well-deserved congratulations. You should be immensely proud."

She smiled her thanks and drank from her glass.

After taking a sip from his glass, Dylan rubbed the back of his neck. "So … ah … what're your plans for the spring?"

She tilted her head and pursed her lips, a crease disturbing her forehead. "I have to pass a nursing exam, then I can apply for nursing jobs either here or in Walla Walla."

Walla Walla? How far away was that? Less than an hour, or more? He'd ask Ethan later.

She studied him, her smile bright and cheerful, her forehead smooth again. "What about you? How long are you planning on teaching at the seminary? Indefinitely?"

He cleared his throat and shoved a hand in his pocket again. "I'd planned to teach through the end of next semester and through the summer if they have need of me. But after Ethan's wedding in August…" He lifted a shoulder. The location of where he would live after Ethan and Lillian married remained a mystery and he'd not yet had the energy to tackle the task of exploring his options.

Realistically, could he afford to live here on his own? Rent in a mountain resort town couldn't be cheap, and he'd never even considered the idea of buying property here. Now, if the seminary offered him a full-time position, he would have more income to work with and a wider array of options.

"There's a parade on Christmas Eve in downtown Trinity Lakes."

"Oh?" He refocused on Jocelyn and drank from his cup again. "I'm sure Ethan will drag me out to that. He loves crowds."

"I'll be there with my brother." She grinned and took a step backward. "I always love standing on the corner downtown where the parade floats turn. Maybe I'll see you there."

He lifted his chin and studied her, mulling over her careful yet casual words. She still wanted to hang out with him. After he'd broken things off.

"Thank you for the drink." Hesitant but with a smile still gracing her face, she waved, then turned and left.

Now he'd be the one dragging Ethan downtown.

———

PARADE DAY HAD ARRIVED and Jocelyn was ready. She'd been ready since six this morning. The two-mile walk from her neighborhood to the corner of downtown Trinity Lakes, where West Wainscott Drive intersected with Main Street and the beautiful old stone bridge that crossed the lake was totally worth it. This corner offered the best view of the parade, and afterward, they could access most of the shops and restaurants —and the lake, of course.

She and Jake arrived half an hour before the parade was slated to begin and already local townspeople, along with tourists, packed Main Street. This is why she'd insisted they walk. Crowds like this meant zero parking and were always a nightmare for emergency medical personnel.

However, Jocelyn didn't have to worry about that today because she wasn't on duty.

Jake surveyed the thick crowd of people, all bundled up against the early morning chill. "Should've brought chairs."

"You'll be fine." Jocelyn refused to let his grumpiness get to her.

"Better yet, we should've driven."

"Where would we have parked?" The nearby parking spots were all blocked off with caution tape and cones. Every street in the neighborhoods beyond had been lined with cars.

Surveying the main through-streets of Trinity Lakes brought a smile back to her lips. Every streetlamp wore twisting bands of green, and some had bows of red or silver or gold tied around them. The shops and restaurants were bedazzled with red and green ribbons. Snowmen and Santas and Nativity scenes graced many storefront windows.

"I forget how all-out Trinity Lakes goes during the holidays." Jake folded his arms with a grumble. "It's like Christmas threw up everywhere."

"I love it." Jocelyn held her gloved hands together and rose on her tiptoes. With snow on the ground, all the bundled-up people and all of the holiday decorations hanging in every doorway, she felt like she'd stepped into an old Thomas Kincade painting.

Now if she could just find a few of her friends. Or one friend in particular.

"You should see Christmas in Sydney."

Jocelyn whirled around to find Dylan standing several feet away, an uncertain smile in that gorgeous beard of his. She desperately wanted to throw her arms around him but restrained herself. "You came."

Dylan's uncertain smile morphed into a grin.

Jake exchanged a glance with Jocelyn then glared at Dylan and Ethan, who stood behind him. "Who are you?"

"Might ask you the same thing, mate."

Jocelyn laughed at the tinge of jealousy in his beautiful Aussie accent. The moment they'd spoken together at her graduation, she knew, oh she knew, she never wanted to forget him or let him go. She'd do whatever it took to be his friend again, even if that meant seeking him out or prompting him to find her.

"Dylan, this is my brother, Jake. He's in town for a few more days."

Jake lifted his chin in greeting.

"Jake, this is Dylan and Ethan. Friends of mine."

Ethan, ever the charming and professional one, extended his hand with a smile. "Nice to meet you." He turned his gaze to Jocelyn. "Good to see you again, Jocelyn."

Dylan shook Jake's gloved hand as well, without the pleasantries.

Ethan read something from his phone, then lifted his gaze with a smile. "If you'll excuse me, my fiancé is looking for me." He ducked out, and disappeared into the crowd, leaving her, Dylan, and Jake alone. Sort of.

Jake glanced between Dylan and Jocelyn again and eyed her with raised brows. She turned away, feigning confusion. Despite all their years apart, she knew exactly what her brother wanted to know. Who was this man, and what was the story between them?

Jake eyed the Bellbird Café storefront across Dylan's shoulder.

"You want some coffee, Joss?"

"Sure. Thanks." She rattled off her typical order and watched him saunter across the street. Would he make it back in time before the parade started?

Dylan moved closer to Jocelyn. "Nice bloke. Even if he was giving me the biggest stink eye I've ever seen."

She laughed, feeling that deep inside. "Dylan, I'm glad you came."

He caught her eye, and for the first time in weeks, he smiled like he had while they were skiing together. Then he glanced away and focused on the myriad of people wandering back and forth, their pace hurried so they wouldn't miss the beginning of the parade. "Are you really planning to apply for work in Walla Walla?"

She turned to study him, but he stood with hands deep in his jacket pockets, avoiding eye contact. "What do you think I should do?"

He shook his head and held up his hands. "I'm not about to stand in the way of your dreams. I want you to be happy, and I know a job in nursing is a step toward your dream."

Her heart soared—he'd unknowingly opened the exact door she needed. "You know what would make me really happy?"

He raised his brows, waiting.

"To be your friend. To take it as slow as we need, and to find out where all this could go." She inhaled, staving off the trembling within, determined to plow ahead. "I know we rushed into things. I realize that probably wasn't wise, but I still want to be your friend because I had the best week of my life with you on that mountain, and I don't want that to be the last thing we remember about each other."

He smiled again, a genuine smile that caused crinkles around his eyes. "All right. We take it slow then."

Her eyes misted, and she turned away. *Thank You, Lord, for another chance.*

At the sound of music from the edge of Main Street, the crowd cheered. She rose on her tiptoes again, searching for her brother. He might not make it back before the parade reached where they stood. But she smiled anyway because she couldn't have picked a better alternative person to stand with.

She turned toward Dylan again. "So will you stop ignoring my texts now?"

He grinned again and rubbed his beard. "I suppose."

CHAPTER THIRTEEN

Dylan stood beside Jocelyn, relishing their time alone together. Fifteen minutes into the parade, her brother—Jake was it?—rushed across the road in between a band and another float and held up two cups of coffee and a bag of pastries.

Settled with his coffee in hand and a pastry in the other, he turned toward Dylan. "How did you two meet?"

He exchanged a glance with Jocelyn, whose eyes danced with mirth. He assumed she'd already told him, or would tell him later, that she'd rescued him in some harrowing mountain rescue, but he wasn't going to be the one to throw that bit out there. "We met over Thanksgiving at the Trinity Lakes Ski Resort." Man, he'd laid the Aussie bit on thick. Wonder if Jake would laugh if he found out Dylan had dual citizenship.

Jake scrutinized him with a creased brow, then turned away and said nothing more while they watched the rest of the parade.

At the conclusion of the parade, they followed the crowd and walked behind Santa Claus's North Pole float until the parade spilled out onto the downtown village green.

A twenty-foot noble fir covered in lights, and hundreds of ornaments and candy canes, took precedence in the center of the village green. Around the tree, food carts and vendors lined the walkways, including a coffee cart with a red striped awning, and a lengthy line.

Ethan and Lillian joined them on the green, and together they all wandered through the green, chatting together as if they'd always been friends. Except Jake, who acted like Dylan wasn't part of their group. What was Jake's problem?

But Dylan paid Jake's behavior no mind. Jocelyn's happiness was paramount, and he suspected from her bright smile and the back-and-forth banter between her and Jake, that having her brother here meant the world to her.

Gray clouds thickened overhead. Ethan stared up at the sky with his brow furrowed. "Smells like snow."

Dylan shook his head with a laugh. 'How do you do that? You can't smell snow."

"Sure, you can." He smiled. "Comes with growing up here."

"Elise did that too. I never could—" Dylan caught himself before he said anymore. He glanced at Jocelyn, but she chatted away, oblivious.

"We'll be right back," Jake said over his shoulder as he tugged Jocelyn across the lawn.

When they'd walked out of earshot, Ethan and Lillian moved in front of him, both with eager eyes and mischievous smiles. "Tell me what happened before we got here," Lillian asked.

What? Dylan exchanged a glance with Ethan.

"She knows everything. Come on, man. You should know that by now."

Dylan ran a hand along his beard. Great. "What exactly do you think I need to tell you?"

"Are you guys together again?" This from Ethan.

Dylan gave a noncommittal shrug.

Ethan laughed. "That's not good enough."

He glanced in between Ethan and Lillian, ensuring Jake and Jocelyn weren't on their way back. "I think we've decided to take it as it comes, see where things go."

This time, Ethan rolled his eyes. "This from the guy who kissed her five days after meeting her."

Lillian gasped and covered her laugh with a hand to her mouth. "Would that be typical?"

"Not for Dylan."

Dylan scowled. "Thanks, mate. Never should've told you 'bout that."

Ethan and Lillian both grinned at him, still sharing a laugh together. Infuriating.

They rejoined Jocelyn and her brother and walked around a bit more, but the lines for food were longer than he cared to endure. He could eat later when the lines thinned out.

Ethan and Lillian said goodbye, promising to see him at the Christmas Eve service tonight. Before they left, Lillian offered him a quick hug and whispered in his ear, "Good luck!"

He rubbed the back of his neck as they left, then turned to find Jake jogging across the green by himself.

"Where's he off to?"

Jocelyn's smile never wavered as she tracked him through the crowd. "He wanted to catch up with a couple of old friends. He hasn't been back in years. I'm sure we'll see him later."

Dylan stepped closer and tilted his head in the direction of the lake. "Want to get out of this crowd?"

Jocelyn grinned and followed him with a bounce in her step.

They spent the next hour taking a leisurely walk along the lakefront and across the large stone bridge over Lake Wainscott. They stopped in the center and gazed out over the stone wall. From here, they could see the shops on the lakefront to the right and the beautiful mountain peaks to the east. The lake shimmered as it narrowed and disappeared into the mountains.

Dylan bumped against her shoulder. "It's as beautiful as I remember it."

"How long have you been away from Trinity Lakes?"

He crossed his arms over the top of the stone wall. "Oh, nearly six years now."

"I came back four and a half years ago." She followed suit and leaned next to him. "What were you doing before you moved to Trinity Lakes?"

"I graduated with a master's while in Sydney, and then did a year-long mission trip in Uganda helping teach English. Afterward, I transferred to the seminary here. Several schools in Sydney coordinate with schools in the US. I'd always wanted to visit the States, so I thought, why not? I met Ethan and then Elise while working on my doctorate."

He waited a moment to gauge her reaction. When she nodded for him to continue, he refocused on the gray waters below. "After my trip to Uganda, I knew God wanted me to continue working overseas. But teaching English wasn't the only thing I wanted to be able to do. I wanted a deeper theological foundation. After I graduated, we married, secured visas, and traveled back to Africa together. We were in Uganda for a year and a half before she passed away."

Jocelyn laid a hand on his arm, and he covered it with his own. "What did you do afterward, back in Australia?"

He tipped his gaze down to her. She smiled, in spite of the somber topic, encouraging him to continue. He cleared his throat. "The first year was most challenging, but my family has remained quite amazing through it all. They encouraged me to use the degree I'd worked so long to obtain."

They would really like Jocelyn. But he shelved that thought for now. She and he *needed* to take things slowly.

He briefly recapped his work as a graduate assistant, adjunct, and associate professor, before Ethan proposed the idea of working here in the States.

Jocelyn's smile brightened. "Seems God has been taking care of you, even through the hard times."

He inhaled a chilly breath and stared out over the lake. "Seems He has." And still, He continued to do so. Gratefulness expanded within, not only for God's care, and for the care of his family, but for this woman, whose first thought was a recognition of God's goodness. He glanced upward into the gray clouds. *Thank You, Father.*

He glanced at Jocelyn again. "What about you? What were you doing before you returned?"

She told him the sordid tale of her ex, and how she wished she'd recognized the signs of cheating much earlier on. Then she recapped what he'd heard before regarding her father's death, but in more detail. She explained how the main reason she'd remained in Trinity Lakes was because she'd inherited his house after his death.

"I didn't mind Trinity Lakes growing up, and I wasn't even gone that long, but coming back home has never felt sweeter. Even before my dad passed, the love and care and compassion toward me from everyone who knew my family, all those people truly revealed God's heart to me. But the sudden loss hit hard. And I decided I never wanted to be in that position again, of feeling so helpless. So, I became an EMT."

Dylan blinked as memories of his own helplessness flooded him, of having to carry an injured Elise two miles down the road before he found anyone who could attempt to help her, not knowing whether carrying her would do more harm than good.

Jocelyn bent her head toward his, her hand still warm against his arm. "Were you telling the truth when you told me you thought I was brave?"

"I meant every word."

White flurries of snow began to fall from the sky, silent in their descent.

Jocelyn gasped and stood up tall, and he missed the warmth

of her body against his. She stared up at the snow, then twirled around and stuck out her tongue.

He laughed at her childlike innocence, wondering if she'd ever be caught doing that while wearing her ski patrol or paramedic uniform.

Then he marveled at each flake as it fell, spiraling downward until it touched the stone and melted away. God's handiwork was truly miraculous, down to the tiniest of creations.

Below the bridge, snowflakes fell into the water and dissipated in an instant. Then more flakes fell and stuck, coating the stone railing in white.

Jocelyn's hand found his, the thin, maroon-colored glove covering her fingers still warm. Snow had collected on her beanie. He brushed it off and smiled. "How are you getting home?"

"Walking. You?"

"I don't have a car here. Only a bike." They'd already walked two miles and who knew how far she lived from here. Although a walk through snow-covered streets sounded wonderfully romantic, he'd not thought to wear gloves this morning.

"Let's find somewhere warm, grab some lunch, and find Ethan and Lillian."

By the time they'd finished eating lunch together, the snowfall had halted for now. Dylan sent a text to Ethan and then offered to walk her home after all.

They strolled in contented silence through postcard-perfect neighborhoods depicting idyllic winter scenes. Though he'd held her hand earlier, he kept his hands in his pockets this time. *Slow and steady. We have time. No need to rush.*

"Will you be at the Christmas Eve service tonight?" she asked as they turned down another street. Quaint houses with triangular-peaked rooftops lined the street, with pines large and small in between.

"I've been meaning to ask, which church do you attend? I'm

thinking it's not the same one as Ethan and I. Otherwise I'm sure I'd have seen you there by now."

"I attend Trinity Life Church over on the eastern side of town."

"Are you attending that service tonight?"

She nodded and led him up the driveway toward her house. "I completely understand if you'd like to go with Ethan tonight."

Dylan rubbed his beard. Everything in him wanted to say yes, of course, he'd go with her. Anything to spend more time together. But attending the Christmas Eve service was a major tradition for Ethan and his family, and he'd anticipated going with them again for the first time since Elise's death.

She stood beside her door, waiting. He stepped toward her, closing the distance between them. "I'll talk to Ethan about it when he gets home and text you later."

She nodded and fiddled with the fingers of her gloves.

He reached for one hand. "What're your plans for Christmas and New Year's Eve?"

"My brother and I are celebrating Christmas together, and then he's leaving the day after. And I work for four days after that. So far, I have no other plans for New Year's Eve. Except …"

She paused and glanced up with sparkling eyes.

"Except what?"

She eyed him directly. "I'd hoped to spend it with you."

He grinned. "I wouldn't have it any other way."

———

CHRISTMAS EVE SERVICE was the highlight of Jocelyn's year. And her brother didn't want to go.

"I never understood why it's so special anyway." He sat on the couch, arms folded, face contorted in a pout like a sullen teenage boy.

She tamped down her disappointment. She'd known he

hadn't considered himself a Christian for years. But this aversion toward Christmas was new. He'd never acted this sour whenever they video chatted.

"It's a most beautiful and amazing feeling when you're standing shoulder to shoulder with everyone in the community. Don't you remember going as a kid?"

He ignored her question and propped his socked feet on the coffee table. "I doubt everyone in town attends."

She frowned at him and then shook her head. He'd missed the point entirely.

She planted her hands on her hips. "What's got you so riled up? You've been a jerk all day."

"Have not." He scowled, sinking farther into the couch. "I came with you to the parade, didn't I?"

She shrugged. After days of not wanting to do anything. And while at the parade, he'd complained and been rude to Dylan and been grumbly and whiny in general. Maybe asking him to room with her wouldn't work out after all.

Jake eyed her. "What's with the Australian anyway? Where did you two really meet? And why does he have a thing for you?"

She couldn't hide a grin as she turned toward the kitchen. She should finish the pile of dishes before heading to the Christmas Eve service.

Jake followed her into the kitchen. "Joss, what are you not telling me? Where did you guys really meet?"

"We met at the ski resort."

"At the bar?"

"No," she snapped as she grabbed a sponge and the bottle of dish soap. She kept her face turned away as she filled the sink with hot water and squirted enough soap to create a rising mountain of bubbles.

Jake stepped in front of her before she could turn to open the dishwasher. "How then?"

She expelled a breath. "I rescued him from the top of a ski run."

"What?" Jake leaned back against the counter and folded his arms. "How?"

She briefly recapped what had happened. Jake laughed, as she expected he would.

"All right. I've told you all the juicy details, now please move."

"Is that why he has a thing for you? Because you rescued him?" He snickered, but finally moved out of her way.

"I don't know, but he's a really nice guy." She collected several cups and placed them in the dishwasher.

Jake leaned against the opposite counter now. "Maybe he is a nice guy ..."

Jocelyn shot him a glare at the skeptical tone in his voice.

He ignored her and continued. "But is it wise to get involved with a guy who'll probably end up leaving to go back to his homeland? All the way across the world?"

She shrugged and returned to rinsing dishes and putting them in the dishwasher. "If it makes you feel any better, we're not dating. We're taking it slow."

"Right. Sure."

But he said no more and moved out of the kitchen. She mulled over Jake's words as she washed the larger pots and pans. Who cared where he came from? He was here now. And he said he had dual citizenship. But that didn't mean he'd stay here indefinitely. He could come and go without having to worry about work visas or anything.

What if Jake was right? What if, after he finished teaching and after Ethan married, Dylan decided to go back to Australia?

CHAPTER FOURTEEN

Familiar faces surrounded Jocelyn, and goosebumps rose on her arms as the congregation sang classic Christmas carols. Words couldn't quite express the warmth she felt emanating from the community surrounding her. While Jake stood silent beside her, at least he was here! He'd decided at the last minute to brave the cold and tag along, if only to keep an eye on her and Dylan. In his words, of course.

Dylan's presence beside her as he stood singing in his enthralling Australian accent, made this night better than perfect. She hadn't expected him to choose her tonight, but he *had*, and joy welled up from within at the thought.

At the conclusion of the service, Dylan held a hand to her back as they navigated toward the exit. Jake walked behind them. "Not dating, huh."

She shot a glare over her shoulder and mouthed, "Be nice."

In the foyer, Dylan shoved his hands in his jacket and waited in silence beside Jocelyn while she greeted friends and introduced him. She took her time and chose her words as carefully as he chose his actions.

A couple of old high school friends called Jake's name from

across the foyer and beckoned him over. Jocelyn smiled. "Go hang out with your friends. You've only got one more day."

He speared her with a knowing glance but sauntered off toward his friends anyway.

Dylan filled in the spot next to her. "Is he always so sour?"

She folded her arms. "I don't know." They video called frequently, but she hadn't seen him much in person since she'd left for college in California.

Maybe this was how he behaved in person? Maybe something had happened recently?

Dylan leaned in close and lowered his voice. "Can I steal you away for a coffee, or does he have you on a curfew?"

She laughed and turned toward the door. "Let's go."

She ignored Jake's tracking gaze as she walked out into the snowy night with Dylan. Once inside her car, with the heater blasting, she texted Jake her intended location and told him to ask one of his friends for a ride home.

Now who's being a jerk?

She ignored his surly text and drove the short distance to a coffee shop downtown.

Once they had warm cups of hot cocoa in hand, she and Dylan settled at a small table in the back corner underneath a single overhead lamp. She leaned toward him and sipped her cocoa.

"How's Ethan? Spending time with Lillian tonight?"

Dylan nodded. "His family and her family went to the Christmas Eve service at Trinity Lakes Community together."

"Was Ethan ever like that toward you? The way Jake is right now?"

Dylan sat back and rubbed his beard. He took his time, maybe formulating his thoughts, as he drank from his cup. "Ethan and I got on quite well. We studied similar topics, though he's older than I am and earned his PhD a couple of years after I began studying for mine." He sipped his drink. "As for Jake's attitude … well, I can relate. I have three sisters back home, and I sometimes wish I'd been there more as they grew up so I could keep a closer eye on the blokes they chose to go with." He grinned a toothy grin.

Jocelyn sipped her drink, Jake's warning pressing itself forward in her mind. *We're just friends, remember?* She struggled to keep her heart from rushing off and falling head over heels like it had a month ago. It was way too soon to be thinking about moving *anywhere* for another guy. They needed time. For conversations just like this.

"Do you have pictures of your family? Can I see?"

He showed her photos of his family from his phone—his three sisters, one brother-in-law, a niece and a nephew, his parents and aunts and uncles—and photos of where he lived, his family's home church, the gorgeous landscape around Australia, mostly from within the city. Listening to him talk about his life back home was both refreshing and unnerving. Would he ever go back without her? She would, if she were him, if only to be with family.

In turn, she pulled up photos of her parents, and her family from when they were younger and together and happy. Her eyes misted as she studied Mom and Dad's faces from before they'd split. Before she'd known there were brewing conflicts. Maybe there always had been. How had she never suspected anything was wrong?

Maybe she should call Mom tomorrow. But she knew Jake wouldn't have anything to do with that. Whereas she'd drawn closer to God during the tumultuous divorce and Mom's subsequent abandonment, Jake had run in the opposite direction, both physically and spiritually, and didn't seem to want to look back.

Later, she dropped Dylan back at his and Ethan's shared residence on the north side of the lake, in a cozy, gated townhouse community located between the bible college and seminary campuses. Before exiting her car, he leaned over and caressed her cheek, then held a hand to her face, with the most endearing and tender gaze. "Be safe driving home."

She gripped the wheel and could do nothing but nod. He was making this friends-only situation so difficult.

"Text me when you get home?"

She nodded again. "It's not really snowing."

"It's dark, and there's snow on the ground." The tenderness in his words warmed her through and through.

"I'll text you."

He exited, then stood and watched as she drove off.

At home, she sent him a text letting him know she was safe, then went in search of Jake. She found him already asleep in the second bedroom, sprawled out on the bed, still in his clothes.

A text pinged on her phone as she pulled on an old sweatshirt before bed.

From Dylan. *Glad you're home safe. Merry Christmas. Sleep well, sweetheart.*

She held the phone to her chest, her heart puddling. What a wonderful Merry Christmas indeed.

———

TREPIDATION CHURNED in Dylan's stomach on Christmas morning as he rode alongside Ethan toward his in-laws' home, located in the hills above Trinity Lakes.

Former in-laws. *Former.* Such a foreign concept to wrap his mind around, though he'd come to accept Elise's passing. While he'd talked to Ethan regularly over the years, he'd only video-called Pearl and Don once a year.

Sitting on the side of the car that he typically would've been driving on still unnerved him, particularly as Ethan drove through the winding mountain roads. Blast, he should be used to this by now. He'd been here since August.

They rounded a corner where the ground sloped sharply downward on the right side toward a winding river, and Dylan gripped the side of his door. "Careful, mate."

"Relax. I've driven this route a thousand times." But Ethan obliged and slowed his driving speed.

By the time they arrived at Ethan's parents' quaint cabin, nestled in the middle of a grove of tall pines, Dylan quickly exited and inhaled several deep lungfuls of fresh, mountain air. He stood in the gravel driveway, blinking as memories assaulted him. Little, if anything, had changed in the landscape.

Ethan lugged a carry bag full of wrapped gifts from the car toward the front porch. "You coming?"

Dylan couldn't move yet. "I need a minute."

Ethan shrugged and turned to greet his mom, Pearl, who waited on the wooden porch.

Dylan leaned against the car, his heart aching.

Nearly four years, and three Christmases now, without Elise, and he recalled none feeling as sharply painful as this one did right now, with the once familiar scene of white snow covering the ground and tree branches, collecting in the gutters at the bottom edges of the high-peaked roof.

His time with Jocelyn yesterday had been incredible. Their growing friendship was a healing salve over the wounds of his past. Right now, he ached to be with her, to have that euphoric distraction.

But is that healthy? Me replacing Elise with Jocelyn?

That wasn't fair to Jocelyn. Truly, he liked her a whole lot, and would never dream of hurting her by constantly holding her up to who Elise had once been. He needed to slow down.

Most importantly, he needed to make things right with himself and his memories of Elise.

Instead of going inside, he pulled down his beanie and walked along the trail behind the house, a trail he and Elise had trekked together many a time, hand in hand. He could almost feel her presence and struggled to endure both the comfort and the pain.

Though her absence was just as stark, he'd avoided all these memories of Elise while in Australia because nothing there reminded him of her. Back home, the missed opportunities hurt the most. That he'd never taken her to Australia before traveling to Africa weighed heavy on his heart for years.

Here in Trinity Lakes, everything around every corner reminded him of Elise. Walking through the campus grounds, walking along the lakefront, eating at the cafés and diners in town.

And walking this trail behind her childhood home.

Ethan's words from weeks ago filtered through his mind. *"For a missionary who traveled into remote villages in Africa, you're awfully skittish."*

The idea of returning to Africa pressed upon his heart like a branding iron. *I know You want me to go back, Lord. But how can I?* Fear clawed in his gut at the idea of returning to the continent where his wife had tragically died. *How can You possibly expect me to do that again? Can't I go somewhere else?*

Footsteps crunched through the snow behind him, and he turned to find Ethan approaching along the trail. "Everything okay?"

Dylan waited, standing with hands buried in his coat, unable to answer. Ethan waited patiently beside him as the silence of the forest surrounded them.

"I didn't think it would be this hard."

Ethan nodded in acknowledgement. "Maybe this is a good thing. Facing the memories."

"Yeah, I thought that too." He rubbed the back of his neck.

Ethan tilted his head in the direction of the house in the distance. "Come on. Mom is worried. We should get back. It's warm inside and there's plenty of food."

Dylan quirked up one side of his mouth. "That only works on you, mate."

But he obliged and followed. Inside, he shed his beanie and coat, but before he could sit, Pearl wrapped him in a warm embrace, then kissed his cheek. "I missed you so much."

Pressure built behind his eyes. He'd not visited after the funeral, and, in fact, had run away so fast he hardly remembered saying goodbye.

He kissed her cheek too. "It's good to see you, Pearl."

The rest of the afternoon, he devoted himself to listening to the stories of his former in-laws, to what they'd been doing for the last several years, and what plans they had going forward. Of course, Pearl and Don were exuberant over Ethan and Lillian's wedding plans and when she arrived later, they greeted her as if she already belonged to the family.

Like he had once belonged.

Well, he still belonged, to a degree, but not to the same level. And if he ever chose to marry again, he'd no longer be part of this family as he had in the past.

Except, in being Ethan's friend, of course.

After a hearty Christmas meal, and when presents had been handed out and opened all around, Dylan found the attention still fully on Lillian. He didn't crave attention, far from it, but being the fifth wheel felt awkward.

Regardless, joy and excitement filled his heart for Ethan, a true friend who continued to engage him, even when he ran off to hide away halfway across the globe.

A ping from his phone sounded and he glanced at the screen. A text from Jocelyn.

Merry Christmas. How are you?

I'm well, and you?

Can't complain.

He smiled as he typed a reply. *Is your brother behaving himself today?*

He made breakfast this morning. It was an unexpected and wonderful surprise.

As an apology? Dylan inserted a winking face at the end.

Maybe. Maybe not. Cooking is his passion. He's a culinary school graduate and works in a restaurant in Texas.

Too bad I couldn't be there instead. To make breakfast and all.

She didn't respond immediately, but then sent a GIF of a woman blushing. Dylan chuckled and pictured her pretty face in his mind with rosy cheeks and kissable lips.

Lillian and her future in-laws were deep in conversation to his left. Ethan leaned close to him to peek at his phone. Dylan held it away from his view. "What are you? A schoolboy?"

Ethan grinned a dopey grin.

Dylan frowned at him. "What's that look for?"

"I'm glad someone has finally made you smile again."

Dylan kept his phone flipped downward to prevent Ethan's prying eyes. "I smile plenty."

"Not like that you don't." Ethan's eyes sparkled with laughter. "Not since you and Elise."

Dylan frowned and mulled over Ethan's observations.

When Ethan finally turned to talk to the others, he turned his phone over to continue his texting conversation.

What do you want to do for New Year's Eve?

Haven't we already had this conversation? Her reply included a grinning emoji.

I know, but what do you want to do together?

Surprise me?

He smiled again and rubbed his beard. He hadn't been back in town in years, but from what he did recall, some of the larger towns nearby put on aerial fireworks displays for New Year's Eve. That sounded absolutely perfect—depending on how far away they had to travel. He'd ask Ethan later.

All right then. We'll make a day of it.

Can't wait.

CHAPTER FIFTEEN

Jocelyn cut a glance sideways to where Jake sat in the passenger seat, silent and engaged with his phone. He'd been more pleasant yesterday, but he'd also ducked out of the house the moment she mentioned she wanted to call Mom.

She bit the inside of her mouth as she refocused on the highway. Was this how all guys handled things, or just Jake?

This morning, the griping had returned as they prepared to return to the airport in Spokane. She'd been tempted to drop him in the closest town with a rental car agency. But he was the only sibling she had.

Time to decipher the root cause behind his grumpy behavior.

"I have to ask you something."

"Hmm?" Jake still typed on his phone.

Jocelyn drummed the wheel with her fingers. "Are you always this grumpy, or is this a recent thing?"

"What?" His gaze shot to her. "I'm being grumpy?"

"Only every waking moment. Especially when it came to Dylan."

He expelled a heavy breath.

"I get wanting to be protective and all, but I felt like it was a bit much."

He remained silent. She cut a glare toward him, then returned her gaze to the road.

"Come on. What's going on? Is it me? Dylan? Being back in town? Some girl drama in Texas?" She forced herself to stop the list of possibilities, though she had other ideas. She'd figure this out. Not like he could go anywhere to get away from her for the next two hours.

"Remember that girl from New Zealand I was friends with?"

She wracked her brain for a face. She'd been gone two years already by the time he graduated high school.

"I'm sorry, I don't." She shook her head.

He huffed another breath. "Well in high school, I dated this girl, originally from New Zealand, who had been adopted by a family here. Long story. Anyway, I had all these plans … like maybe we'd go to college together. Then when she turned eighteen and I was twenty, she decided to go back to New Zealand."

Wow, that was a long time ago. She caught an angry scowl on his face in her peripheral vision.

"She didn't have to go back. She could've stayed here. Her adoptive family was here. But she chose to leave anyway. She begged me to come, but how could I leave? With what money?"

"Did she ever come back? After you left for school?"

He shook his head. "Not that I'm aware."

Jocelyn expelled a long breath. *I'm sure there's more to the story than just Jake's side.* But figuring out the side of the story from a girl who was long gone would not help Jake feel better at this point.

"I'm sorry that happened, Jake."

He barely acknowledged her sympathy before retreating back into his phone. Over an hour later as she navigated off the freeway, a scowl still marred Jake's expression.

"Are you worried Dylan might do the same thing to me?"

"There's no 'might,' Joss. He will leave. And you'll be forced to choose."

Jake's concerns were valid, but she wouldn't allow that fear to stop her from pursuing friendship with Dylan. He'd already become someone she cherished, whether he chose to stay in the States or not.

"Did you stay in contact with her?"

He shook his head and fixed a hardened gaze out the window. "Maybe I should have. But we didn't part on good terms."

By the pained expression on his face, she'd not contacted him either. Poor Jake.

She let him stew in silence for the duration of their drive to the unloading zone. Clearly these emotions ran deeper than what she was capable of wading through.

When they'd parked and he had his bags in hand, she wrapped her arms around him in a hug. "You're my only brother and I love you, no matter what. That's not going to change."

His entire demeanor softened, and he dropped his bags and held her close. "Thanks, Joss."

She stepped back. Emotion caught in her throat, but she pushed it back down. "Thank you for coming to visit. It meant the world to have you here."

Sadness filled his eyes again, as if he hadn't known how deeply she'd needed his presence. "I'm sorry for how I've been. But I'm so proud of you and everything you've accomplished." He hugged her once more, then retrieved his bags.

She watched him walk away and murmured a prayer that it wouldn't be years until she saw him again.

———

DYLAN STOOD on the old stone bridge overlooking Lake Wainscott with Jocelyn wrapped in his arms, pulled close against his chest. New Year's Eve had dawned cold, but clear and blue and beautiful. The perfect day to end the year. He'd taken Jocelyn skiing in the morning and then they'd returned to downtown and consumed way too much food throughout the rest of the day with all the other tourists who'd inundated the small town. Tonight, after eating a light dinner, he had plans to take her to Spokane to watch an aerial fireworks display to ring in the New Year.

For now, they rested, quiet and content, reveling in the beauty of the lake, the town's festive atmosphere, and the snowy landscape around them. Six days without seeing her had left him desperate for this, and he'd waited too many hours already. Finally, they were alone—sort of. He did his best to ignore the mingling locals and tourists who walked or rode bikes along the bridge. Much too cold for riding around, in his humble opinion.

A frosty gust of wind blew against his face, and Jocelyn tucked herself in closer. He smiled and rested his chin on her shoulder while she leaned her head back against him. They faced the west and watched the sun sink lower and lower over the river that wound through an endless expanse of hills covered in evergreens.

"I missed you all week," he murmured in her ear.

She rewarded him with a laugh. "I thought we were supposed to be taking things slow."

"I can't help it." He nuzzled her neck, what he could reach beneath her heavy faux-fur-lined coat, and she laughed again.

He'd spent the entire day holding back, but with every passing hour, his resolve diminished until he knew what he wanted. If only he could tell her.

When he turned to face her, with the intent to capture a kiss, she turned her face gently away.

Sufficiently chastised, he expelled a breath and closed his

eyes. Was this God's way of telling him to wait again, or his own words of wisdom from a month ago coming back full circle? Or both?

"Dylan?"

"Hmm?" He opened his eyes and refocused on the setting sun.

She still rested warm against him, leaning backward against his chest. "Would you tell me if you were planning to return to Australia?"

His breath caught in his chest. How long had this been bothering her? "Of course I would."

She remained silent again.

"What brought this on?" He kept his tone gentle.

"Your family is in Australia." She said it so matter-of-factly, with no trace of anger or bitterness. But she wouldn't have asked if the subject didn't bother her. "If this is going to work between us, I want us to be open and honest about the future."

The call to missions God had laid on his heart burned against his chest again. He opened his mouth, then closed it again. He'd made no decision yet. He wouldn't cause her to worry over something not set in stone.

"All right." His hands sought hers and covered them completely. "How about you? Are you staying in Trinity Lakes?"

She expelled a long breath. "There aren't any openings in the local hospital right now, but I have to take this big nursing exam first and wait until I receive passing results in order to apply." She settled closer into him as light faded from the horizon. "So I have no idea what my plans are. I do know that I either need a roommate or more income sooner than later. I've run through most of my savings while going back to school, and this is the first time I've been without a roommate in years."

He rested his chin on her shoulder as she leaned her head back against his opposite shoulder. "Then I guess we're back at square one."

She smiled up at him briefly, then returned her gaze to the horizon.

The desire to kiss her reared up again. He tamped it down. "I'm not planning on going anywhere anytime soon." He would find a way to stay.

"I'm exhausted, Dylan." She closed her eyes. "I know you wanted to go watch fireworks tonight, but the drive to Spokane and back is long and I'm already so tired."

She'd been tired since before they'd eaten a late lunch after returning from the ski resort. Probably due to working four long days then going skiing this morning. And walking around for hours afterward. *I should've chosen a less strenuous activity. Not planned so many things in one day.*

"I'm sorry, Dylan."

"No worries." He ran a hand down the top of her head and through her hair. "Why don't I take you home?" Maybe a nap would do. Then a light dinner and a movie. To him, it didn't matter what they did, as long as they were together.

"I drove you, remember?"

She still lay against him with her eyes closed. He dropped a kiss to the top of her head. "You can re-familiarize me with how to drive on the right side of the road. Then maybe someday I'll return the favor and teach you to drive on the left." He turned her around and gently guided her along the bridge, her arm threaded through his.

She hummed at that.

"Now's as good a time for me to learn as any, as it seems you'd fall asleep if you tried driving yourself. What with having to drop me off then drive back home and all."

"Fine. I'll let you borrow my car. Just make sure you bring it back in one piece tomorrow."

"Of course." He smiled, incredibly tempted to kiss her for real this time. "Just another excuse to drop by and see you."

She laughed as they joined hands and walked back to where

she'd parked on Main Street. Without resistance, she allowed him to drive her the short distance home. Taking a few minutes to learn what he needed to know about her car, and to orient himself to driving on the right side again helped bolster his confidence. Having a car with local controls made it easy.

By the time they entered her house, she really did appear like she would fall asleep standing up.

"I think I'm getting sick." She flipped on the light and the heater, shed her coat and gloves, then collapsed on the couch and leaned against a huge couch pillow, her beanie and scarf still on.

She could be right. That would explain her sharp dip in energy. Must be more than strenuous activity. They'd both walked a fair amount around town after skiing this morning too, but he wasn't nearly so tired.

Gently, he unwound her scarf and pulled her beanie off. He set them aside and went in search of a blanket. Once he found a quilt, he laid it over her, and she stretched her legs along the length of the small couch.

"You sure you'll be all right?" He pulled off one boot, then the other.

"Mmm." Her eyes closed and she smiled a peaceful, beautiful smile that made him want to stay. "I just need sleep."

He ran his hand over her forehead and felt the warmth. His fingers brushed through her hair. "Do you want your skis now?"

"In the morning is fine," she murmured.

He should give her some medicine for her fever, but she probably wouldn't take it given her already half-asleep state. After ensuring he had her keys, he leaned down to caress her warm forehead again. "I'll be back in the morning then. Call me if you need anything at all."

She mumbled a response and was on her way to dreamland before he even walked out the door.

CHAPTER SIXTEEN

Jocelyn blinked gritty eyes open at the sound of children crying. Bright light surrounded her, streaming hot through a broken window. She pushed herself off a low cot and surveyed the tiny room. Her heart pounded. Where in the world was she?

She scrambled backward at the sight of herself in a t-shirt and shorts. What was happening?

Another woman burst into the room in a wide-eyed frenzy. "Have you come to help?" She spoke in a desperate tone, with a thick English accent.

Jocelyn tried to answer but her words never made it out of her mouth. Then the woman turned and rushed off as abruptly as she'd appeared.

———

Jocelyn woke midmorning, her throat as dry and raw as sandpaper. After digging a thermometer from the depths of her bathroom cupboard, she took her temperature.

A fever and sore throat. And a weird dream? What a fun way

to start the New Year. But she'd worry about the dream later. She'd chock it up to being sick. Ugh. First thing, she needed hot lemon ginger tea. Then something to eat. Then she'd call Dylan. Or maybe text.

He beat her to it, having already texted her twice. The second one indicated he was on his way over with her car.

Though she insisted Dylan didn't need to stay, he remained anyway and brought with him ingredients to make soup. He must be the sweetest man in history. If she didn't feel so cotton-brained, she'd have kissed him silly.

But they were supposed to be taking things slow, right?

Right.

Except when he served her hot chicken soup and a hot cup of tea to go with it, her heart puddled at her feet. And whenever he gazed at her with a dopey grin on his face as if she were the only person in the world, she couldn't imagine life without him.

Ease up. You've known him for six weeks, maybe. And you weren't even together for half that amount of time.

But his actions were so caring and honorable. Never once did he verbally entertain the idea of staying overnight. Though he very well could have and she wouldn't have cared. If she were honest, she probably wouldn't have noticed.

In fact, he seemed to be keeping his distance physically—maybe because of her illness. But her brain was too muddled and too overwhelmed with gratitude to decipher the reason. None of that detracted from his kind and caring actions throughout the day.

Two days passed in the same manner. After she'd eaten lunch the next afternoon, they sat together on the couch watching some action movie from her on-demand movie collection. She sipped from a fresh cup of tea, her legs resting across his lap. She could get used to this.

He ran a hand along her leg. "Are you feeling better?"

"Much." She smiled, her hands wrapped around the warm

mug of tea. If only he could come by and do this every single day. She'd never known what she was missing. "When do you go back to teaching?"

"Not for another two weeks." He winked.

She expelled a breath. "I have to work tomorrow."

"Can't you call in sick?"

She mulled over that. "If I'm still sick."

Halfway through the movie, she abandoned her pillow and curled up in his arms. Hang being sick and all the unwritten rules of we're-taking-it-slow. She missed his warmth. His arms were inviting and safe, like what home had been through her childhood. She snuggled in deeper.

In another moment, he caressed the top of her head. She blinked her eyes open to find the credits rolling. What? How much time had passed?

He flipped off the TV, but his arm remained around her shoulders. "When is your nursing exam?"

"Mmm." That was the last thing she wanted to talk about.

"Jocelyn." This time, he laid a hand over hers, which rested against his chest.

"Next weekend." She should be studying but exhaustion clung to her like a weighted blanket.

"Any local job openings you've seen?"

"Mmm mm." She closed her eyes. "Too sick to look, remember?"

He tipped her chin up and waited until she opened her eyes. "Whatever you decide to do and wherever you decide to go, please don't hold back pursuing what you've been working toward for years because of me."

Her eyes misted under the intensity of his gaze. What if that was exactly what she wanted to do? If she left town for a nursing career, she risked losing this. Him.

He kissed her forehead again. The tender gesture warmed

her heart through and through. "Promise you won't put your life on hold for me."

She rested against him again and listened to the steady beat of his heart.

Without realizing it, she'd fallen asleep again, and woke to him kneeling before her. For the second time, he laid a blanket over her, flipped off the lights and disappeared out the front door.

A day more, and she'd recovered her energy enough, but her sore throat persisted, as stubborn as an unwelcome neighbor visit.

Still, she had to work, and she had to study for this stupid exam. And she had the first SAR team meeting of the year tonight. If she could get through a full workday, she could sit through the short meeting. She loved Search and Rescue, almost as much as she loved being a paramedic. Helping people is what she did and who she was. With school over, she'd have more time to commit. Surely, they'd take her back.

Jesse caught her eye as she entered the Trinity Lakes Community Center building that evening. He stood in the hall outside the small room where the SAR team met for monthly briefings.

"I didn't see your name on the team list, so I didn't think you were going to show." His dimpled smile matched his teasing tone.

"I'm only a couple minutes late." She cleared her throat, then dug in her purse for a bottle of water.

Jesse's brow furrowed. "You okay?"

"Getting over a sore throat." She took a drink of water, then headed for the door.

Jesse partially blocked her path. She furrowed her brow. "Wait… what team list?"

"Did you fill out the new application?"

She shook her head. "Should I have?"

He rubbed the back of his neck. "A new director took over the team after you left, and he made all the current team members fill out new applications. The deadline was January first."

She pursed her lips. "I never received any information."

He cleared his throat and his gaze skittered away. "I was afraid that would happen. I emailed you a copy back in November just in case. I should've checked with you while we were at the ski resort. I'm sorry."

"Oh." She expelled a breath. She'd been so busy during the last month of school, what with graduation and the whole dating-Dylan-not-dating-Dylan, and then transitioning back to full-time work again. "I'm sorry. I've been swamped." She drank from her water bottle again. "So I'm out because I missed the application deadline?"

Jesse's brow remained crinkled. "I can try to put in a good word. He mentioned taking new applicants every six months."

She inhaled a deep breath. Fine. This was all volunteer anyway.

Regardless, disappointment swirled within. She'd enjoyed working with the other SAR team members in the past.

Jesse's brow furrowed. "I'm really sorry, Joss."

"Hey, it's okay. It's not your fault. No big deal. I just started full-time work again after two years of working part-time during school, so maybe it's not the best thing for me to jump back into this kind of commitment." She turned toward the exit. "I'll catch you later."

A hand on her arm stopped her mid step. "Hey, you still coming rock climbing with me? How about in two weeks? I'll pay your way. For your birthday."

She smiled over her shoulder. "That sounds fun. I'll see you then."

"Looking forward to it."

———

DYLAN SAT across from Jocelyn at the Bellbird Café for lunch after church the next weekend, enjoying a meat pie. Jocelyn stared at him while he ate. He grinned at her curious, bemused expression. "Want to try?"

She screwed up her face. "No, thanks."

"It's not that bad." He laughed. "You can't know what you think until you try it."

She shook her head and continued eating her boring sandwich with lettuce and tomato and cheese. He chuckled again, glad to see her back to her normal, energetic self.

"Did your exam go well yesterday?"

She shrugged while she chewed, then spoke once she swallowed. "I think it went all right. I'll find out in a few weeks."

He nodded. Good. She'd spent most of the last week studying and had to drive to Walla Walla yesterday to complete the five-hour test.

"I do have some news." She ate a bite of a dill pickle, then continued. "The human resources lady from the community hospital attends my church, and she told me in passing today that the hospital would love to hire me—depending on my test results, of course."

"This is great news, Jocelyn." He smiled.

She held up a hand. "But I won't know for a few weeks."

He waited for more of an explanation.

"She says one nurse is pregnant and may be going on maternity leave in May and another nurse is set to retire soon."

He smiled again. "I'm excited for you. You've already come so far."

She smiled that shy smile he adored and covered her face for a moment. Dropping her hand, she caught his gaze again. "Thank you for believing in me."

He reached for her hand, refusing to acknowledge the keen

glances in their direction from two servers as they passed. Let people believe what they wanted. Only Jocelyn's opinion mattered, and she didn't once pull her hand away. Nor had she shied away from his affection while he'd taken care of her after New Year's.

Her eyes lit up as she took another bite of her sandwich. "I forgot to tell you. One of my ski patrol friends works as a rock-climbing instructor at an indoor adventure park. He invited me to visit next weekend. Would you want to come with?"

He nodded, stifling an unexpected and unwarranted ping of jealousy. Of course he would go with her. "That sounds fun."

What could possibly go wrong?

CHAPTER SEVENTEEN

A faux-rock formation loomed in front of Dylan and Jocelyn as they stood inside the adventure park where Jesse worked. Kids and adults clustered together in groups with instructors along the bottom, while a handful climbed along the rock wall itself.

Jocelyn grinned, then glanced sideways and found Dylan staring at her, wide-eyed. She surveyed the rest of the room along with him, admiring the massive open space with its lofty ceilings. With rope ladders, giant jungle gym structures, rope bridges, and a zipline that began in the back corner and spanned the length of the building, it was like a giant playground for adults.

Jesse approached, wearing a helmet, with climbing harnesses slung over his shoulder. "Hey, welcome!" He grinned. "Right on time."

Jocelyn glanced at Dylan and noticed his cautious but polite smile. "Jesse, this is Dylan Mackay. We met at the ski resort. I texted you he was coming with?"

He shook Dylan's hand. "Glad you could make it."

"Dylan, Jesse grew up in Trinity Lakes, and we've worked

together on the mountain rescue team and on the ski patrol for a few years."

"You still live in town?" Dylan stood with hands in his pockets. She'd come to recognize that as an observational, if a little guarded, stance.

He adjusted the ropes and harnesses slung over his shoulder. "I'm in Walla Walla for now. But my granddad lives in the mountains outside of town, and I visit him a lot."

Jesse gestured for them to follow him toward the giant rock wall. As he led the way, he glanced backward and eyed Jocelyn. "Did you want to free climb or use a top rope?"

"I'm good with a rope today."

Jesse laid down the harnesses he'd been holding. While Jocelyn pulled on and secured her harness, Jesse focused on helping Dylan with his. Then he pointed out the ropes hanging from pullies above and explained how the process worked.

"If you want to climb together, I can grab another guy to hold the second rope. For now, let's let Jocelyn climb first."

Once she was hooked up to the rope and her helmet fastened, exhilaration surged through her as she found her footing and climbed upward. She scaled the first route with ease, then rang the bell at the top. She cheered, pumping a fist in the air.

Dylan observed with his usual quiet and proud smile from the bottom, while Jesse cheered. Once she repelled down to the floor, Jesse laughed and high-fived her. "I should've known that'd be too easy for you. After Dylan climbs, I'll take you to a harder route."

She unhooked her rope. "Give me whatever you got."

"Let Dylan go first."

Next, Dylan climbed cautiously, taking his time as he moved up the face of the wall.

Jesse leaned toward her while keeping an eye on Dylan's progress. "Isn't he the guy you helped rescue?"

She grinned at Jesse's observation. "Yes."

"Who would've thought." Jesse eyed her briefly, then refocused on Dylan, keeping a tight hold of the rope.

"He's a professor at the theological seminary in town. Can you believe that?" She folded her arms and continued to watch. Jesse shouted out pointers to Dylan when he got stuck about halfway up.

When Dylan recovered his footing and continued upward, Jesse glanced sideways again. "Are you two dating?"

Jocelyn huffed out a breath. "Have you been talking to Renee?"

He laughed, a teasing, knowing look in his eye. "Maybe. But it wouldn't have been necessary, not after seeing you two together."

She folded her arms. How could she answer that when she didn't really know herself? Well, half the church congregation would call them a couple, given he'd begun attending her church and sat with her every Sunday now. He'd been as attentive as any boyfriend, but he hadn't tried to kiss her again since New Year's Eve. And he hadn't held her close like he had when she'd been sick. He would reach for her hand once in a while, and it felt as natural as breathing to walk beside him with her hand in his. But other than that …

Jesse raised his eyebrows. Oh, she hadn't answered him yet.

"We're taking things slow."

Jesse snorted. "Okay." He focused on Dylan as he neared the top. "Isn't he from Australia?"

"Yes."

This time, Jesse focused on her directly. His relaxed grin drained away. "Aren't you worried he'll end up leaving?"

She shrugged off the concern. Why everyone worried so much about whether Dylan was sticking around in the US or leaving for Australia was beyond her. In this era, staying connected was as simple as a video call, even if they were on opposite sides of the globe.

When Dylan reached the top, he cheered and she cheered with him, clapping her hands. "Great job!" She whistled.

Setting his feet against the wall, Dylan pushed off and rappelled down. Somewhere along the line, Jesse must have given Dylan rappelling instructions, because he handled his descent just fine.

When his feet touched the ground, she closed the distance between them and wrapped her arms around him. He held her tight against him. "Great job, Dylan!"

"Thanks." He grinned from ear to ear as he unhooked the rope from his harness. "What a blast."

"All right. Now for a challenge." Jesse approached with a mischievous grin. "You and me."

Oh, no, what crazy idea did he have up his sleeve?

Jesse led them around the corner to the other side of the rock formation. Here, the rock holds were much smaller and farther apart, the route more of a zigzag pattern than straight up. She folded her arms.

Jesse grinned. "To make it even more fun, I thought we could race."

She resisted rolling her eyes. He'd beat her by a whole minute, she was sure. But she never backed down from a challenge. "You're on."

Two of Jesse's co-workers appeared and held the ropes while she and Jesse secured their harnesses. She eyed him, grinning. "Are you trying to prove something? Because everyone knows you've been climbing much longer than I have."

"This is just like in high school."

She laughed outright. Had he really been holding against her the fact that she'd beat him in a little rock-climbing contest while they were in high school? "That was how long ago? And I was two years older."

"And now it's time for a rematch." But his wide, mischievous grin belied the seriousness in his tone.

"This hardly compares." She gestured to the difficult route in front of her.

He said no more and approached the wall, ready to climb. She cast a glance at Dylan, who stood to the side, observing with an amused sparkle in his eye.

She followed Jesse and tried to map the route she wanted to take in her head as she approached. On his "Go," she quickly found her footing and began her ascent.

Of course, he was always a hold or four ahead of her the entire time.

Reaching the top proved more challenging than the first climb, by far. Concentrating on not falling or slipping off the tiny grips left no room for conversation or bantering as she tried to catch up to him. But Jesse was fast and tall and agile and flexible, and what had she been thinking in the first place? He worked here full time, although he likely didn't do a lot of climbing on the job unless climbers got stuck. Still, he practiced climbing with search and rescue, too.

Apparently, a small crowd of people had gathered at the bottom, as evidenced by cheers and clapping that erupted when he reached the top. He didn't even bother to ring the bell as he sat on the top ledge waiting for her.

When she finally reached the top, he wasn't smiling, not exactly. Whatever. She was too tired to process that weirdness. Whew.

She rang the bell though and pumped a fist in the air. Who cared if she got second place? That route was hard.

The crowd below erupted with applause again, and then dispersed. She glanced at Jesse. "Congratulations. You made that look easy." She wiped her forehead.

He smiled, genuinely this time, but still sat as if he wasn't ready to go back down yet.

She breathed out a long breath and shook out her arms. She hadn't been climbing since last summer. "Are you even tired?"

He chuckled. "A little bit."

"So does the winner get anything? You never named a prize for this little wager."

"I can't name the prize I want with Dylan down there." He glanced downward. "But I'm glad I could treat you for your birthday, even if it is two weeks early."

She frowned and stared at him. What was that all about? "How about I buy lunch? You deserve it."

"Sure." He fist-bumped her shoulder. "Good job. You kept up with me most of the way."

She wasn't so sure about that, but she'd take the compliment.

———

A SECOND-LEVEL DECK in the middle of the huge indoor adventure park housed a café of sorts, with typical lunch and snack bar fare. Dylan let Jocelyn pay for Jesse, as per their rock-climbing wager, but he insisted on paying for her, and she didn't argue. At least the wager had been good-natured, though Jesse had been less celebratory than he'd expected. Which seemed strange. Maybe it wasn't about beating Jocelyn, but about proving he could do the hardest route. He looked fit enough to do it ten times over.

They sat down together with sandwiches, fried chicken, and a large tray of fries to share. "I take it you two knew each other growing up?" Dylan gestured between Jesse and Jocelyn, who sat across from each other.

"Jocelyn's brother and I were closer in age, so we hung out sometimes. Joss left for college during my junior year in high school, then my parents pulled us out and left Trinity Lakes halfway through the year." Jesse munched on a fry.

Jocelyn nodded as she ate. "Don't feel bad. Most kids left after high school anyway."

They chatted back and forth about where they'd gone to college. Dylan ate in silence. Sure, he could talk about going to uni in Australia, but that would lead to mentioning attending graduate school here. He'd rather not bring up Elise. That would be a conversation killer.

"How long have you been rock climbing?" Dylan asked Jesse during a lull in the conversation.

He shrugged. "A few years."

Jocelyn laughed. "Try like since you graduated high school!"

Jesse offered a humble smile.

"I should've forfeited." She munched on a fried chicken strip. "I'd hardly even call it a contest."

The temptation to reach for her hand welled within. Instead, Dylan kept his underneath the table. "Then you wouldn't have known what you were capable of."

She shrugged. "I guess."

"That was a hard climb. You did great, Joss." Jesse eyed her with a serious expression of what Dylan could only interpret as admiration. He tamped down his jealousy. These two had history, yes, but so far, Jesse had presented himself as professional and courteous to both of them.

Jesse turned toward him. "How long have you been a professor?"

Well, that wasn't any better of a topic, but he wouldn't be rude. He finished chewing. "A friend of mine told me of an opening here. I began teaching in August."

"You came all the way from Australia to work in Trinity Lakes, Washington?"

"Well, I attended seminary here years ago." He paused, formulating the right words that wouldn't involve his grief-stricken past. "After I moved back to Australia, my old mate and

I kept in contact. He's getting married, and he invited me to come back to teach for a while before the wedding."

"That's pretty cool." Jesse smiled while he ate.

Jocelyn leaned forward. "Jesse, how is your grandpa?"

Dylan expelled a breath of relief as Jocelyn guided the topic in a new direction. Affection welled from within. How was he so lucky to have met another woman who had come to know him so well in such a short time?

Since they'd driven a fair distance and Jesse had paid for full day passes, Dylan and Jocelyn spent the rest of the afternoon climbing rope ladders and walking along rope bridges while Jesse worked. Dylan let Jocelyn cajole him into ziplining. Sure, he'd done some ziplining as a kid back in Sydney, but nothing as intense as this one situated at least two stories high. The rush of it was terrifying and exhilarating all at the same time. Jocelyn's giddy laughter and screams as she followed behind him made it worth the temporary fright.

As they prepared to leave, Jesse met them at the exit to say goodbye. Dylan offered a hand to shake. "Thanks for inviting us. I'm happy to pay you back for the cost of the day."

He shook his head. "Don't worry about it. It was my gift for her birthday. I'm glad you both came."

Jocelyn stood next to him and bumped his shoulder, but her eyes were on Jesse. "I had so much fun, Jesse. Thank you."

He nodded and smiled. "See you when I see you."

"See you when I see you."

In the car, as Jocelyn drove, Dylan mulled over how to approach her past history with Jesse. If he didn't ask, it would bother him the rest of the night. So far, honesty had been the best policy during their relationship, so he forged ahead with that in mind. "Is he an old boyfriend or ..."

"No." She shook her head. "Well, he never asked me out." She leaned back as she drove. "I hardly talked to him at all when we were kids, not until I returned to Trinity Lakes. I met him my first year on the SAR team. He doesn't live in town. He stays with his grandpa sometimes and probably has a season pass for the ski resort."

Dylan released a slow breath of relief and reached for her free hand across the console dividing them.

"So you don't have anything to worry about." She cut a sideways glance his way and smiled that smile he'd come to love and adore. A smile that softened her entire face and illuminated her eyes.

A smile that made him think for certain she felt the same way about him as he did about her.

CHAPTER EIGHTEEN

Dylan tugged his beanie down as snow fell around him, silent and beautiful in its serenity. He bent down and wiped a layer of snow off the surface of Elise's gravestone, revealing her full name, date of birth and date of death.

Pine trees with bits of snow stuck to their branches guarded the small graveyard, tucked into a southern corner of hilly land just out of town, somewhere between the access road that led to Lake Other and the turnoff for the main highway.

Many of the graves sat on rolling hilltops, with views of the town and the three lakes to the north, west and south. But Dylan focused only on the simple marker bearing Elise's name. He blinked hard against the burning in the back of his eyes.

They'd had so much to look forward to. How could she have died so young, before the age of thirty?

Footfalls crunched in the snow behind him. He pushed to stand, brushing snow off his jeans.

Ethan stood silent behind him, a thermos of something in his hands. "You found it all right, I see."

Dylan nodded and shoved his hands deep in his coat pockets. "The groundskeeper somehow knew where to look."

"I meant the actual property, but yeah, graves can be tricky to find in the dead of winter." Ethan drank from his thermos.

"I remembered how to get here." He hadn't recalled much from the funeral and burial—hadn't wanted to remember— but once he'd found the correct turnoff for the graveyard, he'd recalled what the entrance looked like. Not that there were any other buildings around, just a nondescript single-story building in the forested hills. "Thanks for letting me borrow your car."

Ethan nodded and fixed his gaze off into the distance down the hill. "Mom and Dad are following me, but they offered to give us some space."

Dylan glanced behind him. That was nice of them. "I appreciate that."

Ethan pulled out a paper with distinct creases, as though it had been folded and refolded multiple times. He blinked rapidly as he opened and read the letter in silence. Afterward, he cleared his throat, then offered the letter to Dylan.

"What's this?"

"The last letter I got from Elise before she died." Ethan rubbed his eyes.

Elise's last letter?

Dylan took the letter, holding it as if it were some ancient document, as much afraid to touch it as he was to read it. "You don't have to give this to me."

Ethan turned away. "But I want to."

Dylan skimmed the first few lines, then tore his gaze away. Reading words she'd written so long ago would wreck him, no matter what they said. His first instinct was to crumple it up to keep himself from enduring the pain—but the letter was precious to Ethan. He wouldn't have kept it if it weren't important, and it wouldn't be in this frayed and fragile state.

"I can't … I'm sorry, Ethan, I can't."

A tear tracked down Ethan's cheek. He wiped it away. Without speaking, he walked off, hands in his pockets, toward the bluff that overlooked one of the smaller lakes. He stood for a long time, staring off into the sea of pines.

Dylan was such a coward. *God, why do You even bother with me?* He held the letter as gently as possible, folding it along the worn creases. Ethan's parents arrived, and Dylan nodded at them. All three stood at the foot of her grave in reverent silence.

Ethan rejoined the group and embraced his parents without words.

After a time, Pearl and Don turned to leave, arm in arm. Ethan followed, and Dylan fell in step beside him.

"I'm sorry, Ethan. Please, take it back. The letter's yours."

Ethan's tears had cleared, and he focused ahead of him with a resolute expression. "Will you read it before I get married? As a wedding gift to me?"

"Really?" Dylan frowned and swallowed against the lump in his throat. What a strange request. "What's so important about it?"

Ethan stopped and turned toward him. "Please."

Dylan released a heavy breath. Odd request or not, that would give him several months to muster up the courage. "All right."

Ethan continued again, following his parents across the snow-covered grounds. "Come to lunch with us?"

Dylan nodded. "Thank you. I'd like that."

***

ON THE SUNDAY before Valentine's Day, Dylan searched for Jocelyn after church. He'd been attending Trinity Life Church for several weeks now, and had noticed as of late, a particularly joyful smile would light up her entire countenance whenever he appeared beside her. After crossing that four-year mark without Elise, Jocelyn's radiance acted as a healing balm to his tender heart. From the moment they'd met, her positive, energetic, face-anything personality made him want to be brave again.

Today, as he approached, her grin ignited the beautiful forest-green of her eyes. After she said goodbye to her friends, she turned to focus solely on him.

He held his hands in his pockets. "Sorry, I was running late today and ended up in the back."

Her gentle smile remained. "I'm glad you're here."

He cleared his throat. "Are you doing anything for your birthday today?"

Her eyes widened, still bright and cheerful. "You remembered."

He winked. "Someone may have dropped the exact date to me." And he'd be eternally grateful. Missing the chance to celebrate her actual birthday would have been a huge step backward, especially after Jesse had paid for a full day at the adventure park.

She held her coat close in both arms. "To answer your question, I am free all day."

He grinned. Perfect. "Will you come on a lunch picnic?" His hand begged to reach for hers, but he shoved them both into his coat pockets instead. "I might not see you on Valentine's Day." If that little confession didn't show her how he felt, he'd likely have to be even more direct. "I thought we could venture into the mountains. What do you think?"

To his utter delight, she needed no convincing and eagerly offered to drive.

The surface of the lake shone bright and gorgeous and blue with hints of white as they drove by, reflecting the perfect sky above with its puffy white clouds and the evergreen trees surrounding much of the shoreline. The snow had melted down in town and everything shone beautiful and green.

Cutting south out of town, Jocelyn followed his directions

up the old mountain highway that wrapped around and veered north, toward the ski resort.

"Just so you're aware," Jocelyn glanced sideways at him "I was wrecked the last time I went skiing after working four days in a row."

"Don't worry. I have other plans." He grinned, captured her free hand, and squeezed it once before releasing it.

It'd been six weeks since New Year's Eve. Since he'd tried to kiss her again. Dylan's desire to take things further had increased with sharp intensity in the last two weeks, but other than hand-holding, he'd stuck to taking things slow as they'd decided.

But with every passing day, certainty expanded within until he could hardly stand it. She made him want to officially call Trinity Lakes his home all over again.

Snow covered the ground as they drove farther into the mountains, but the trees remained green and tall, flanking the road.

He directed her to turn down a small road before the ski resort turnoff. The lane ended in a packed parking lot. Two families dressed in snow clothes walked across the pavement, towing children on sleds behind them.

Jocelyn laughed. "A snow park?"

"I've never been." He couldn't stop grinning, even if he'd wanted to.

Jocelyn parked and gathered her coat. "I didn't even bring my hat and gloves."

He opened the back of the car and pulled out the duffel he'd brought and opened it to reveal several beanies, two pairs of gloves and snowpants for each of them, along with lunch foods he'd packed. The wide-eyed smile of surprise she gave him was reward enough for his sneaking around.

Once they'd gathered what they needed, they walked toward

the set of stairs that had been dug out of a bank of snow. Jocelyn gripped his arm. "We don't have any sleds."

"Already thought of that." He led the way toward a small building where a line had formed.

He rented two sleds, and they tromped through the snow together, following other families. They spent the next half hour racing each other down a huge hill, climbing back up, then racing each other down again.

As he stood on the top of the hill for the third time, his breath escaping in puffs of fog, Dylan eyed a father and son as they slid down the hill on a sled together. He grinned at Jocelyn, whose rosy cheeks glowed in the sun. "Want to ride together?" He gestured toward his sled.

"We can try." Giddy with laughter, she shoved her sled upright in the snow so it would stay, then climbed on the front of his sled. She dug her feet into the ground to keep it steady as he climbed on behind her.

He wrapped his arms around her, and all the memories of their first week together flooded through him. "I could get used to this."

She laughed and shoved the sled forward with her feet. "Put your feet up, or we won't make it very far."

Frigid air rushed by as they flew down the hill, faster and farther than they'd gone before. But when they tried to turn left to avoid a high snowbank, the sled wouldn't cooperate.

Dylan sucked in a sharp breath as they neared a small embankment at the wrong angle. In another moment they were flying up in the air and over the hill then crashing downward into powder. Jocelyn shrieked as the sled flipped sideways, dumping them off together in a heap. Dylan found himself lying on his back, covered with cold snow.

He lay still, his eyes closed, heaving to catch his breath. Jocelyn's joyful laughter rang in his ears.

And I thought ziplining was a rush. He'd prefer not to do either one of these things again anytime soon.

"Dylan?"

He kept his eyes closed, breathing deep. Ow ouch. *Getting too old for this.*

"Dylan? Come on, get up."

He wanted so desperately to smile at the hint of worry in her tone but forced his face to remain as neutral as possible. But the cold snow seeping through his coat collar and sleeves might ruin the moment.

He flinched as she touched his forehead with a cold snow-covered glove. "Dylan, stop playing around. Are you hurt?"

He smiled and opened his eyes to find her staring straight at him with a mixture of laughter and concern in her eyes. Her hair brushed against his face as it hung from beneath her beanie. "I think I have a concussion."

"You do not!" She burst out laughing.

"I could, you know." He wrapped his arms around her and rolled her over into the snow, until he lay on top of her. She shrieked and tried to push him off, all the while giggling uncontrollably. He silenced her with a quick kiss, and then a not-so-quick kiss. She tasted sweet and chilly and beautiful, like snow and sun together, and he never wanted this to end.

She ran her gloved fingers beneath his beanie, then through his hair, and then she swiped his beanie from his head.

He broke their kiss. "Hey, now. That's not nice."

Silent laughter brimming in her eyes, she used the moment of shock to scramble out of his hold, leaving him breathless.

CHAPTER NINETEEN

Giggling and shivering simultaneously, Jocelyn ran—trudged—back up the hill with his hat. She could hear Dylan's heavy footfalls and heavy breathing as he chased her up the slope.

"Jocelyn." His sing-song tone only elicited more laughter. "Give me back my hat."

She cut to the right toward a copse of evergreens, and when she finally reached the trees, he lunged, caught her around her waist, and pulled her close again.

"That's my hat." His voice in her ear sent a shiver of delight down her spine.

Her uncontrollable laughter was her undoing, but instead of recapturing his beanie, he captured another kiss. The warm and delicious and oh-so-delightful sensation kept her trembling at bay. He pulled her closer, moving them out of sight behind a large pine tree.

Breaking apart, she bent her head against his chest to catch her breath. "How long have you been waiting to do this?"

"Much too long. Since the last time I kissed you." A deep

chuckle rumbled in his chest, and he enveloped her completely in his arms. "But it was worth the wait."

Yes, it certainly was worth the wait. She'd not forget this birthday surprise anytime soon.

"I'm freezing." Even though she stood wrapped in his arms, rolling around in the powder had resulted in snow going down the back of her jacket and coating her hair.

"I can certainly fix that." He dusted off the excess snow from her shoulders and jacket, then he kissed her again, his intensity continuing to drive away the chill.

At last, he relented—good thing, because she was out of breath from running in snow and from that series of amazing kisses.

"How about some hot chocolate to warm you, hm?" He pulled his beanie back on and reached for her hand.

After retrieving both sleds, they turned them both in at the rental desk, and returned to the car. Jocelyn opened her tailgate and found two blankets she kept in the car during the winter. They sat together on the tailgate, bundled up in blankets, and Dylan handed her a thermos and a wrapped sandwich.

Jocelyn leaned into him, sipping from a thermos of hot cocoa. Delicious and warm, just what she needed. "You thought of everything."

He chuckled and tapped his thermos against hers. "Happy birthday." He stole yet another kiss.

Mmm. She could get used to this.

"Are you warmer now?"

She leaned her head on his shoulder. "So much warmer."

After finishing lunch, they drove back home, holding hands whenever possible. Gone were the reservations and parameters they'd set before the New Year, which had been slowly fading anyhow.

"I have more surprises for you." He smiled and brought her fingers to his lips.

She giggled, feeling like a college first-year student all over again. "Does it require more driving?"

He nodded. "And a bit of dressing up."

She rolled her eyes but smiled. "I suppose. For you."

"Come on. It's been two months since the last time I saw you all dressed up." His eyes sparked with mischief.

She pulled in front of his home. Before exiting, he swiped her phone. She eyed him as he typed into her phone. "What're you doing?"

"Plugging my birthdate into your contact info." Smiling, he handed it back to her, then stole one more kiss. "Now you know mine."

This time, she kissed him before he could leave.

He ran his fingers through her hair and gently held a palm to the side of her face. "This time, I'll pick you up. In proper dinner-date style."

"About time," she teased.

Dropping his hand, he backed away and slid from the car. After grabbing his bag of snow gear and leftovers from lunch, he appeared in her driver's side window. "See you tonight at five?"

She nodded with what she knew must be the sappiest smile on her face, and watched him walk inside.

At home, she showered and then dug through her closet in search of the only two dresses she owned. At least that made the decision of what to wear that much easier. Her dress chosen, now she had to do something with her long, flat hair. She huffed a breath into the full-length mirror hanging on the back of her door. She hadn't dressed up for a guy in so long.

In the middle of attempting to curl her hair, her phone rang, announcing a video call. From her brother, no doubt. He always called on her birthday. She set the phone against the bathroom mirror before answering. "Hey, I'm glad you called!"

Before he could even say hi, Jake's eyes widened, and his

expression changed to something like … amusement? Happiness? Wariness? She couldn't quite tell.

"This is something new." He smiled, genuinely, now from his position on his couch. "Going somewhere special?"

"Dylan's taking me to dinner." She grinned as she attempted another curl with her curling iron and didn't care how ridiculous it looked.

"That's great, Joss." He reclined into the corner of the couch. "I mean it. I can't remember the last time you got all fancied up for your birthday."

She huffed and attempted another curl. "I've gone out with friends before."

"But when's the last time you dressed like that to go out with your friends?" He winked and his eyes sparkled. "I'm happy for you."

"Thanks." She tried not to frown into the mirror at her hair, she never practiced curling enough to get it right. Hopefully, it looked all right to everyone else.

"By the way, I sent you a gift in the mail. Let me know when it arrives."

"I'll keep an eye out." She finished the last curl and set the iron aside. Picking up the phone, she focused on him directly. "Since you called, I have a question to ask."

A loud *roof!* interrupted the conversation as a big black puppy jumped up onto the couch, disturbing Jake's camera.

"Zuzu sends birthday wishes too." Jake grinned.

Jocelyn cooed and studied the cutest eyes ever. The big black nose bumped up against the camera. "Is that a black lab?"

"Yeah, just picked her out of a litter last month."

Jocelyn smiled as the pup walked around Jake's lap, then finally settled down into a curled-up ball. How cute.

"What did you want to ask me?"

"Would you consider moving back to Trinity Lakes? I could use a roommate." She sat on the edge of her bed.

His cheer diminished as he stroked the dog along its back. "I don't know, Joss. What reason is there for me to come back? Everything I care about is gone. Except you, of course. You can't afford the house on your own?"

She shook her head. "This house wasn't cheap when Dad bought it, and the mortgage is hard to afford alone on a paramedic salary. That's one reason I pursued nursing. I've had roommates off and on, and the last one moved out at the end of October. So far, I've found no local job openings, so I might have to take a job in Walla Walla."

He snorted. "That's not a terrible commute."

Okay, so living in a small town had spoiled her rotten when it came to commuting. "But it would be difficult in the dead of winter." She combed fingers through her hair, careful of her new curls. "I don't want to leave Trinity Lakes. I don't want to leave this house. I don't want to sell it to strangers or manage renting it out."

He pursed his lips. "I'll consider it. But no promises."

She nodded. "That's all I ask." After they said goodbye, Jocelyn finished getting ready. A knock on her door had her scrambling from her closet. She pulled open the front door and invited Dylan inside with hardly a glance. "I'll be back in one minute."

On stockinged feet, she returned to her room. Where had those boots gone? She dug behind a stack of boxes and then a stack of tubs. Ah, finally. When had she shoved them back into the corner?

She slipped them on, then grabbed her purse and rushed down the hall to find Dylan standing at the entrance where the hall met the living room.

He looked as handsome as he had in December at her graduation, in slacks and a black peacoat, his hair and beard neatly trimmed and combed. Her heart raced at the intensity in his eyes as he approached her and ran his fingers through the waves she'd struggled to create in her hair. "You look stunning."

His fingers in her hair felt amazing. She opened her mouth to voice how long that had taken her, but his eyes captured hers, leaving her speechless.

Too soon, he dropped his hand and led them outdoors.

To her surprise, he'd reserved a table at a small, intimate Italian restaurant in Walla Walla. She loved Trinity Lakes, but there was something special about getting away to a fancy restaurant out of town.

After they'd ordered and handed off their menus to the server, Dylan reached into his pocket and retrieved a square velvet box. "I have a Valentine's Day slash birthday gift for you."

Jocelyn covered her mouth. He didn't. He couldn't be... could he?

"I know this might not be entirely practical for your line of work, but I couldn't resist." He smiled and rested the gift in the middle of the table. "I hope there'll be more occasions where you can wear it." He winked and nudged it farther toward her. "Perhaps on more nights like this." Her heart melted at the giddy and boyish grin on his face as she cradled the gift in her hands.

She carefully opened the box and found a shimmery tennis bracelet nestled inside, with heart-shaped, pale pink pearls. "Oh, it's beautiful. Thank you."

He reached forward, unclasped it, and latched it around her wrist. "Perfect for you." He brought her hand to his lips. "Happy birthday, Jocelyn."

She leaned forward and kissed him again, her heart overwhelmed with gratitude and joy. Could life get any better than this beautiful moment?

CHAPTER TWENTY

Dylan hummed a cheery tune as he strolled across the campus toward Ethan's office on the morning of Valentine's Day. The bitter cold of winter had finally given way to signs of spring, though the official start of the season was still over a month away, and Jocelyn's face floated in the back of his mind every time he closed his eyes. What a refreshing vision to dwell on.

He'd taken Jocelyn out last weekend because he hadn't expected to see her today since she had worked a twelve-hour shift, but then she'd texted him this morning suggesting they meet up at the Bellbird after her shift. He couldn't wait.

He found Ethan's office door open, sauntered in, and set his laptop bag and coat on the small couch Ethan had somehow squeezed into the back corner. Ethan sat at his desk with his laptop open, oblivious to his arrival.

"Hey, mate," Dylan said. "Have you eaten yet?"

Ethan glanced up, a smile on his face. "I ate earlier, but thank you."

"Right then, I'm going to grab something." He turned toward the door.

"On second thought, I'll join you. Give me a minute?"

Dylan waited while Ethan finished something on his computer. Then he locked his office, and they walked down the hall together toward one of the small lounges and a small on-campus eatery.

Ethan cleared his throat. "I ran into the Eternity Missions rep the other day."

Dylan stopped in his tracks, but Ethan kept walking.

When Ethan glanced behind him, his usual cheer faded. "Come on, Dylan, please don't do this avoidance-shutdown thing. You haven't even heard what all I've got to say."

Dylan folded his arms over his chest, skepticism searing through him. "What have you got to say, then?"

Ethan planted his hands on his hips. "Would you listen if I told you?" He raised both eyebrows. "To the whole thing?"

Dylan inhaled a deep breath. The burning in his heart returned full force and the impression God needed him to listen, right here and now, sat heavy as an anvil on his chest. He nodded once.

Ethan narrowed his eyes and folded his arms, then continued. "I ran into the Eternity Missions rep on Friday, and he mentioned that one of their teaching missionaries is talking about retiring from overseas fieldwork due to personal and family health problems. Eternity Missions remembers you, and he asked how you were doing."

Dylan's heart trembled. He tightened his arms around his middle.

"He asked if you'd be interested in a short-term mission trip, to see if you're a fit for the location and all they're looking to cover. The trip would be fully funded."

They wanted to send a fully funded missionary into the field? That was certainly fast-tracking things. Usually, a prospective missionary would have to go through an entire application process that took months, with more months spent trying to raise money to fund the overseas work. Foregoing all that was no small thing.

A heap of questions came to mind, but he voiced the most important one first.

"What's the timeline? When is this missionary supposedly retiring?"

"Within the next six months."

"Where are they wanting to send someone?"

Ethan hesitated and Dylan's heart plummeted. *No.*

Ethan stepped forward, holding Dylan's gaze. "To Uganda."

He turned away and retraced his steps toward Ethan's office. Lucky he had a key, or he'd leave his things and head back home.

"Dylan, wait."

"I don't appreciate my best mate pretending to go to lunch with me just to try and convince me to go back into the mission field."

"Dylan."

As Dylan approached the door, Ethan placed a hand on his shoulder and halted his steps. Then he rounded and stood in front of him.

"It's because I am your friend. I know this call has been laid on your heart. I remember the zeal and passion you had before-hand, when …"

"That was then, and this is now." He pushed past Ethan and unlocked the office door himself. "I'm not going back to Africa." How could Elise's own brother ask him to do the one thing that gave him nightmares even now?

"Do you still feel that call?"

Dylan pushed into the room and snagged his briefcase and laptop bag, avoiding Ethan's piercing gaze.

"And would you go somewhere else, or would you ignore the call altogether?"

Dylan shook his head and closed his eyes. He'd had such a

fantastic morning. Why did Ethan have to bring up anything even remotely related to Africa, let alone Uganda?

He turned around to find Ethan leaning against the wall with his arms folded, partially blocking the exit.

"This isn't the Dylan I know. The Dylan I know is courageous and zealous. The Dylan I know ran after God with all his heart and listened when God called him. In fact, that Dylan told me he still felt God's call on his life in spite of all the tragedy. Eight months ago, he told me he wanted to move forward again because he felt stuck. And he traveled back here for a second time, to take a step forward."

"I didn't think it would be this hard." Dylan raked his fingers through his hair.

"Of course it's going to be hard." Ethan waved a hand in the air. "You've relocated to the town where Elise grew up, where you were married. You're working with staff who have been missionaries, students who might be pursuing missions, teaching at the same school you and Elise graduated from. At what point did you think this would not be hard?"

Dylan sank onto the couch and leaned forward, his head in his hands. Every word Ethan spoke rang true, yet fear raced through his veins at the thought of stepping foot in Africa again, whether south Uganda or anywhere else.

Ethan expelled a heavy breath. "If God is calling you to go back out into the mission field, this is a door wide open. But no one is going to force or demand you do anything."

Dylan lifted his gaze to find Ethan's expression engulfed in sadness.

"The only reason I told you is because I thought maybe this could be your chance to move forward again. Because watching you from across the world, stuck on pause for the last several years, broke my heart." He turned toward the door and gripped the knob. "I'm sorry I upset you. That was not my intention.

This choice is completely up to you. I won't say any more about it."

Then he left Dylan alone without another word.

———

A QUAINT SERENITY covered Trinity Lakes this morning as Jocelyn and her two accompanying EMTs, drove through town in between calls. The streets were clear, but patches of snow still covered the ground here and there. The lake beside them glistened under the rays of the rising sun. So much quiet, punctuated only by the contemporary music that Sean, her twenty-year-old EMT driver, insisted on playing, left ample room for Jocelyn's thoughts to wander.

Having Dylan cancel dinner last night left her unsettled. Maybe he truly hadn't felt well, but the last-minute raincheck didn't feel authentic.

On top of that, she'd had that weird dream again, where she woke up in another country. The dream was always the same. The sunlight streaming in felt hot against her skin. Children were crying, and a woman with an English accent always asked Jocelyn if she were here to help. And it would always end with the lady leaving before Jocelyn could answer.

Having the same snippet of dream every so often for the last six weeks had piqued her curiosity. Never in her life had she had repetitive dreams like this.

The meaning of the whole thing rolled around in her mind like a pinball in an old pinball machine. After analyzing the short snippet she surmised she was waking up in some kind of medical clinic outside of the US, what with the doctor rushing in and all.

Was God calling her into medical missions? She'd done a nursing degree with missional emphasis at the seminary purely because it was less expensive than online programs, allowed her to remain local, and the program promised flexibility for working adults. Sure, the idea fascinated her—serving overseas, doing what she loved. Sounded like a great adventure. But right now, she wasn't ready to leave Trinity Lakes. Not at all.

Had this program, with his specific missional emphasis, been part of God's plan all along? She had hoped to talk to Dylan about the dream last night, but of course that didn't happen.

Sean's hand landed on her wrist out of the blue. She jerked away and glared at him. What was his problem?

He smiled, disarmingly, and pulled back his shoulders. "Didn't mean to startle you. Where'd you get that sparkly bracelet?"

She scowled. "Next time, ask first instead of grabbing." She refocused on the road in front of them. Twenty-year-olds were so annoying.

"Where've you been, Sean? She's dating an Aussie now." Grace, an older EMT, said from the back. "It's probably a gift from him." Gracie snickered good-naturedly.

Jocelyn's phone vibrated in her pocket. Typically, she ignored calls during the workday, but the lull in active emergency calls gave her the opportunity to at least check the caller ID.

Jesse? What a weird time for him to call. In fact, he rarely called her at all. They generally communicated via text.

Sean threw a fleeting glance behind him at Grace. "Since when did she start dating?"

"Since the end of December. Word's been all over town. At least downtown. You know people have nothing else to talk about besides who dates who."

"We weren't dating in December." Jocelyn's frown remained in place. "Keep an eye on the road, Sean."

Jesse called again. Jocelyn frowned. Something must be wrong.

"That's funny. I saw you two downtown on New Year's Eve.

Looked like you were dating to me." Grace's singsong teasing tone coaxed a smile from Jocelyn.

"It was complicated back then."

Grace laugh-snorted.

Sean flicked a glance at her then refocused on the road. "So, are you official now? What with the pretty gift and all?"

Jocelyn shrugged. "Yes?"

Grace laughed again.

"Why are you wearing jewelry anyway?" Sean glanced her way again and Jocelyn scowled, tempted to take the wheel from his hands and drive instead. "I thought we weren't supposed to wear jewelry on the job. Work hazard and all that."

"It's the day after Valentine's Day," Grace leaned forward toward Sean. "Leave her alone, will you?"

"I'm just curious." Sean's obnoxious grin reminded her of her brother's whenever he teased her as a kid.

As they rounded a sharp corner, a full-sized doe leapt into the middle of the mountain road. Jocelyn shrieked. "Sean, watch out!"

CHAPTER TWENTY-ONE

The brakes screeched, and the ambulance slid and spun on the icy road. Sean let out a curse as the back of the ambulance collided with something hard. Jocelyn jerked forward, but her belt yanked her back hard against her seat.

Heart pounding, she inhaled deep breaths. Once everything fell into an eerie silence, she opened her eyes. "Everyone okay?"

"I'm okay." Grace's voice shook, but she wouldn't lie, not in her line of work. "I don't think the back of the ambulance is though."

Sean held his head in his hands. Jocelyn unbuckled herself and gripped his shoulder. "Sean? Are you okay?"

"Yeah." His tone, however, did not sound reassuring.

Grace's head poked into the front seat. "Only one of the back doors will open."

Jocelyn expelled a heavy breath. "Keep an eye on him while I assess the outside. Contact dispatch."

Jocelyn walked around the perimeter of the vehicle. The back corner of the vehicle had slammed into a tree two yards from the edge of the road. Part of the bumper, rear light, and side panel were crushed inward, but the tires appeared intact.

Things could've been a lot worse. *Thank You, Lord, for keeping us safe.* Though the tree had stopped their momentum—thank God for that—part of the ambulance still protruded onto the lane. Her heart continued to pound. They had to move the unit before any vehicles came around the bend.

She knocked on Sean's window. "I'm driving."

Sean stared at her, wide-eyed, but didn't argue. He scooted over and re-buckled.

"Grace, is he okay?"

"Physically he's fine, but he's really shaken up."

She would be too, had she been driving.

"Another unit is on its way here. Can we actually drive this thing?"

"I really hope so." She inhaled another deep breath, closed her eyes, and murmured a prayer. Then she turned over the engine and pulled slowly and carefully forward off the snowy grass and dirt.

"How bad is the damage?" Grace's head poked into the front seat again. "Did we hit the deer?"

"I didn't see the deer at all. The back corner of the unit hit a tree when we spun."

On the floor, her phone vibrated against the floorboards. Sean picked it up. "Who's Jesse?"

Jocelyn snatched her phone and answered the call. "Hey Jess?"

"Are you busy right now?"

His shaky tone indicated her instincts had been right.

"What happened?"

"Can you come by?"

"Jesse, are you hurt?"

"I'm not, no. But I think my grandad passed away in his sleep."

Oh no. She released a heavy breath. "Text me your address."

"Joss, we're still parked in the middle of the road." Grace's panicked tone snapped Jocelyn out of her worry for Jesse. She set her phone on a phone mount on the console so she could read and navigate hands free while she drove. After a little skidding on the icy asphalt, the ambulance moved forward along the road without further incident. Facing east, Jocelyn accelerated up to the speed limit, continuing to pray that a tire didn't blow out.

"Where are we going?" Sean folded his arms tight.

Grace sat back and buckled up again. "Are we really going on a call right now? We can't even get anyone in and out of the back."

"Call dispatch and have the other unit meet us at the address I send you." After copying Jesse's address to Grace with a couple clicks, Jocelyn set the GPS on her phone to direct them to Jesse's granddad's cabin.

Sean frowned. "Jocelyn, where are we going?"

"We're going to help a friend in trouble."

———

HALF AN HOUR LATER, Jocelyn sat with Jesse in the living room of his grandfather's rustic cabin. Jesse curled forward with his head in his hands, his fingers gripping his hair.

Emotion clogged Jocelyn's throat. Over the years, she'd learned how close Jesse had been to his grandfather. After his family had moved out of town, Jesse visited annually and sometimes stayed with his grandfather during the winter months. He'd worked at the ski resort off and on but eventually chose to work a full-time job in Walla Walla a couple of years ago.

Jocelyn spoke into the silence of the room. "Sheriff is on his way."

Jesse nodded and scrubbed his eyes with two fingers.

"Did you call your parents?"

"I called them right after I called you. They should both be here by the end of the day." He sat up and scrubbed his face again.

"I'm so sorry, Jesse." Jocelyn clasped her hands together. The entire situation rang with stark familiarity. Sitting in the living room, staring at the other paramedics and EMTs, having to make all of the most difficult phone calls of her life all in one day.

She'd dealt with this kind of pain acutely. And it was more than the grief of losing someone. For the rest of his life, Jesse would wrestle with being the one to find his grandfather eternally asleep. She could attest to how distressing that felt. "Is there anything else I can do?"

"You being here is enough. Thank you." He pushed to stand and stood in silence for a moment, his face distraught, his demeanor so uncharacteristic in comparison to the easygoing young guy she'd worked with on the ski patrol and search and rescue team.

After a moment, he walked toward the door, grabbing a heavy jacket on the way. "Let me know when the sheriff arrives."

After he walked outside, she excused herself from the rest of the EMT and paramedic staff, rose and followed him.

He stood frozen in the middle of his long, plowed driveway where both ambulances had parked, one behind the other. He walked toward the damaged one she'd driven here and studied the crushed back bumper.

"Jesse?"

He turned toward her and stared hard, eyes intense. "Were you in an accident on your way here?"

She closed the distance between them. "Before you called."

"And you still drove here?" He blinked at her, eyes widening. "How could I not?"

His hands reached up and cradled her face. "But are you okay? Are you hurt?"

She shook her head, her heart trembling. This shouldn't be

happening. He wasn't supposed to be acting as if her life were more important than the death of his grandfather. Maybe there'd been some merit in Dylan's suspicions about Jesse's interest in her.

"I'm fine."

"You promise?"

On normal calls, she kept her emotions carefully tucked away and in check, then took time to process everything after her shift ended. But this wasn't a normal call, and Jesse wasn't some stranger having a horrible day. "I'm more worried about you, Jesse."

"That's not an answer to my question."

Without hesitation, she wrapped her arms around him. He reciprocated and held tightly to her.

"You shouldn't be here." He rested his chin on top of her head and she could hear the emotional hitch in his voice.

"How could I not come?"

"Let me amend that." He released her and stepped back, creating plenty of distance between them. "I shouldn't have called you."

"Jesse." She inhaled a shaky breath. Understanding sank in. He'd wanted her here for personal reasons, not just because she was a paramedic.

"I'm sorry. I know I'm overstepping." He turned and continued walking away from the house. "I'll be okay. You should go back to work."

As he spoke, Sheriff Thompson's patrol car turned onto the drive. Jesse directed his steps toward the approaching vehicle and met with him as he parked and climbed out.

Jesse and the sheriff walked inside together, already in deep conversation. The other paramedics and EMTs climbed into the working ambulance, and Jocelyn climbed into the damaged one. The county coroner would be out later today.

She and the others returned to their headquarters near the

hospital and spent the next hour filling out paperwork. Her boss offered her, Sean, and Grace the day off.

She hated sitting around alone after traumatic calls. Doing nothing wreaked havoc on her mentally, but her boss was right. Going back to work right now was not a wise idea.

Before leaving for home, she called Dylan.

CHAPTER TWENTY-TWO

A familiar Trailblazer sat on the curb in front of her house. As she parked, Dylan climbed from Ethan's car and met her at the door. He greeted her with a tender kiss and a gentle smile.

"Thank you for coming." Though the haze of today's events still clouded her mind, just having him here raised her spirits.

"I'm sorry I missed going out with you last night." He held his hands to her face, like Jesse had done. Except Dylan's gentle touch brought a welcome and exhilarating warmth. "Are you sure you're all right?"

"I'm okay, I promise." After her encounter at Jesse's, she'd pushed the accident to the back of her mind. But the similarities between the two men's actions had her stomach twisting in confusion and guilt—even though she'd done nothing wrong. She turned away and unlocked her door.

She invited him in, flipped on lights, and eyed his empty hands. "No laptop bag? No grading today?"

He shook his head. "Did you have lunch yet?" he asked as he hung his jacket on the arm of the couch.

"Not yet." She entered the kitchen to investigate how much

food she had left. Honestly, she wasn't confident she had anything to work with in the fridge, as she ate out most nights and tended to eat breakfast for lunch on her days off. No one would know it, as she put in a thirty-to-forty-five-minute run or bike ride when she woke up.

Dylan met her in the kitchen and wrapped his arms around her. Her heart melted as he dipped his chin close to her ear. "Let me cook for you."

She smiled and agreed, then crashed on the couch while he cooked. She could get used to this.

Later, as they were finishing a plate of chicken and pasta he'd somehow finagled out of her limited ingredients, she noted how quiet he was while they ate. Or maybe this was his normal demeanor, and she'd always been the one making conversation, filling in the silence.

He reached for her hand and squeezed it. "How is Jesse fairing?"

She offered a half shrug but didn't answer. She hadn't heard from Jesse since she'd left, and didn't expect to, not after how they parted. Eventually, he'd text her an update. But a line had been crossed and things weren't going to be the same going forward.

"Thanks for lunch." She smiled, then walked her dishes to the sink.

Dylan met her on the couch, and she welcomed his embrace. "How's your driver?"

She rested against his chest and listened to his heartbeat. "Sean was pretty shaken up afterward."

"Speaking from experience, accidents are tough to handle when you've got others' lives on the line." He caressed the top of her head. "How about a movie to take your mind off all this?"

She covered a yawn with a hand to her mouth. "Sounds good." Any kind of distraction sounded fine by her. Her adrenaline from the morning seemed to seep away from her with every passing minute.

With her still held firmly in one arm, Dylan navigated the TV menu until he found a movie to watch.

Halfway through, a knock sounded at the door.

She walked to answer it and found Jesse standing on her doorstep. "Hey, Jesse."

"Hi, Joss. I ..." He gripped the back of his neck. "I was wondering if ..." He glanced behind her, then shook his head. "Never mind. I'm sorry. I should've called instead."

She glanced behind her and found Dylan standing three feet back. She stepped outside and closed the door for a moment.

"You're here now. Tell me what's up?"

He shook his head again and backed away. "Never mind."

She followed him as he walked back toward his car. "Jesse."

He turned around again, his hands shoved deep in his jacket. "I came to say goodbye. I'm not sure when I'll be back in town since I used to stay at Grandad's. It's been less than a day, and my parents are already talking about how the cabin should've been sold years ago." A hint of bitterness dripped from the last statement. "They'll be here later this afternoon. Already booked to stay at the Lakeview Inn because they could never stand the cabin."

Jocelyn moved closer. "So ask them to give it to you instead."

He shrugged, but his downcast expression revealed his skepticism in that idea. "We still have to go through all his things and see if he left a will or a trust or something."

"Weren't you renting some place in Walla Walla?"

He nodded once. "The lease is about to expire, and they want to raise my rent significantly, so I had planned to move back in with Granddad for the foreseeable future. Clearly, I'm going to have to find something else now."

Had he come looking for a place to rent? She could use the

income. "I don't mind you staying here. I'm gone so much of the time anyway—"

He held up a hand and shook his head. "Joss … please don't."

She opened her mouth, then closed it again.

"You know I can't do that. Don't make this harder than it already is." He raked his fingers through his hair. "I respect you entirely too much to come between you and another guy."

"You wouldn't." Jocelyn swallowed a rise of emotion. "But I understand." She rubbed at the burning in the back of her eyes. Who knew when she'd see him again?

Jesse kept his hands in his pockets. "I'm happy you're happy. Let's leave it at that." He cleared his throat and fixed his gaze off down the street, where thin patches of snow still covered the ground here and there, and bare trees stretched toward the sky. A picture-perfect image of a slice of life in Trinity Lakes.

"Will you be back?"

"I love this town. That's why I've visited so much." He expelled a heavy breath. "It's too soon to tell." He swung his gaze briefly back to her. "But I hope. Someday."

She closed the distance between them and gave him a quick hug goodbye. Then he climbed in his car and left, and she found tears trailing down her cheeks.

———

DYLAN SURVEYED the scene unfolding outside on the lawn through a crack in the door with unease churning in his stomach. He'd sensed something was off when she didn't want to elaborate on Jesse's state of mind after his grandfather's death this morning. Jesse's downcast expression and demeanor portrayed how deeply bothered he was, and explained why he was here seeking out Jocelyn in his vulnerability.

Jesse showing up unannounced, combined with her downcast mood, and all the doubt and fear that Dylan had wrestled with for the last day, worsened his unease.

With every passing hour, the assurance that God wanted him to pursue this opportunity Ethan had presented solidified in his soul. Of course, He never specified whether the opportunity would work out. This was a test. A test to see whether Dylan was willing to listen to God's promptings, regardless of what the outcome might be.

Coming here today only confirmed how deep his feelings ran for Jocelyn, which further complicated God's prompting on his life. Regardless of her mood. In fact, these vulnerable and sad moods left him never wanting to leave her side.

God, how can You truly ask me to leave, right now, where I'm at?

After her conversation—and embrace—with Jesse, Jocelyn turned to head back indoors. Dylan retreated from the doorway and waited for her to return.

She wiped her eyes as she entered and shut the door.

"Everything all right?"

She gave a half-hearted shrug and returned to the couch. Before she could sit, he reached for her hand to stop her progress. He chose his first question carefully. Accusing her or assuming anything at all, would get them nowhere. "What's happened?"

She studied him for a beat in silence. "Jesse had been living with his grandfather, but now he has to find another place to stay. He came to say goodbye."

Had he been looking to stay at Jocelyn's house? Dylan rubbed his chin.

She sniffled again and then sat on the couch. "His parents are coming into town. Staying at the bed and breakfast. He says they've never liked the cabin." She exhaled a shaky breath. "I'm sure he'll be fine."

But she didn't appear fine.

He sat next to her and held onto her hand. She cut a sidelong glance his way. "Dylan, you don't have anything to worry about." She attempted another half-smile.

Dylan wanted to trust her words, but from where he stood, he had his doubts, what with the tortured expression on Jesse's face as if he were sorry he'd missed his chance.

The death of a loved one was no small thing, and vulnerability drew out the deepest emotions in anyone. Dylan couldn't fault Jesse for his decision to come here, not after what he'd endured.

Still, jealousy lingered, tainting his spirit of compassion.

Dylan brought her hand to his lips. "I'm sorry his grandfather passed away."

"Me too." She leaned her head on his shoulder.

Dylan caressed her forehead, then turned the movie on again.

By the time the movie ended, she'd nearly fallen asleep on his shoulder. He kissed her goodbye and rose from the couch.

Before he could leave, she reached for his hand to stop him. "Promise me you won't worry about Jesse and me?"

He tilted his head, uncertain of how to answer that request without lying.

She stood and wrapped her arms around him. "I care about you, Dylan."

"And I you." He rested his forehead against her hair. "I'm glad you're all right."

After one more lengthy kiss goodbye, he finally walked outside to his car.

The weight in his heart lifted at the image of her smiling as he left. She'd resolved to choose him and only him. That was all well and good—a huge relief. Now, how was he supposed to resolve his own issues of whether to stay in Trinity Lakes or pursue mission work overseas?

CHAPTER TWENTY-THREE

March brought with it cold nights and beautifully sunny days that hinted at spring. This afternoon, the lake glistened in the sun from Dylan's view atop one of the hills on the seminary campus. He spotted a handful of sailboats and kayaks out enjoying the water. Too bad he had two more classes to teach today. A bike ride along the lake sounded perfect right about now.

He finished the coffee in his travel mug and navigated along the footpaths back toward the building where his next class would be so he could prepare for his students.

"Dr. Mackay?"

Dylan turned to find a young man hurrying down the path toward him. He waited until the man caught up. "Can I help you?"

"My name's Andrew. I've got a couple of friends in your morning classes." He smiled and adjusted his laptop case over his shoulder. "I wondered if you had a few minutes to talk missions?"

Dylan nodded once and led the way back toward the small cluster of buildings. "What would you like to know?"

"I read your bio online, and some of the articles you've posted in the Eternity Missions magazine. I've heard a little of your story, and wondered if you had any advice about going on a long-term mission trip for the first time?"

Dylan studied the man as they walked. Tall, willowy. He looked a bit bookish with his glasses on. A gold wedding band gleamed from his left hand. Where was he taking this line of questioning?

"Well, the desire to go into missions can stem from many things. For me, I felt a strong and resounding call from the Lord. For others, it might be more a set of open doors, combined with career skills they've picked up. Have you been planning for something like this, or do you feel called?"

"I've felt called for years. I participated in three mission trips in high school and during my undergraduate years."

Dylan nodded. "Tell me about them."

Andrew talked about how his youth group had gone to Mexico and Trinidad, and how he'd traveled to Ukraine during college, before the war. Then he cleared his throat. "I know your wife passed away, and I'm very sorry for your loss… but if it's not too uncomfortable, I wanted to ask, what are your thoughts on couples going into missions together?"

Ah, there. That was the root of Andrew's concern. Oh, Dylan could relate to the feelings of uncertainty, both right now and when he and Elise had been newly engaged. The prospect of going into missions was such a personal thing, yet when married, it became vitally important to ensure you and your spouse were on the same page when making decisions.

"Let's sit and talk." Dylan led them to a table near the main building where they could sit in the sun. Then he told his story, of how incredibly nervous he'd been approaching Elise with the proposition of going into missions together so soon after being married, of how it was simultaneously both blissful and incredibly difficult, of the dangers of everyday life living in Uganda, and of the car accident and Elise's subsequent death.

Afterward, Andrew blinked back a sheen of tears. "Thank you for telling me your story."

Dylan nodded again and passed Andrew his business card. "I know this is a difficult decision. I highly recommend prayer. Together. Lots of prayer over the matter. If you decide to apply for a long-term mission trip, call me and we can talk more."

Andrew nodded and thanked him again, tucked the business card away, and said goodbye.

That night, Dylan sat in his kitchen and stared at his laptop with most of his dinner uneaten beside him.

Two weeks had gone by since Ethan had approached him with the proposal to take on this missionary opening. Every day he'd felt the tug to take this leap of faith, more and more. And nearly every day that he taught on campus, some student or another approached him with a question about missions. Apparently, he had become a popular person of knowledge on this topic, which wasn't his intention when arriving in August.

Andrew's zeal while he recapped his previous mission trips reminded Dylan of how he'd felt eight or nine years ago. Familiar peaks of excitement had gradually begun to return to his heart, even now.

But Jocelyn ... he had still yet to discuss any of this with her.

What if he passed on the Eternity Missions contact information to Andrew instead? *Can You send this young man in my place?*

When no answer came, Dylan rested his head against his laptop. Of course there would be no easy out. Maybe Andrew wouldn't take his place, but Dylan could still pass his name on to Eternity Missions regardless.

Ethan came home and sat across from him. Quite unusual, as he usually stashed his things in his room and exchanged his collared button-up for an old t-shirt. Dylan closed his laptop and moved his dishes aside. "What's up?'

Ethan crossed his arms over the tabletop. "I know I said I wouldn't mention it again, and I never intended to put any pressure on you, but the Eternity Missions rep has been bugging me every day for a week, saying he's feeling strongly led to set up a meeting with you and the other missionary. And I've tried putting him off and explaining what happened—"

"Go ahead and set it up."

Ethan blinked at him with his mouth open.

"It's only a meeting, right?" A meeting wasn't a commitment. If anything, a meeting would serve to help him gather information to send to this other young man. Just in case.

A broad smile lit Ethan's face. "I'll have him call you." He stood as if he didn't know what to do with himself for a few beats, then disappeared to his room as he usually did.

Dylan closed his eyes again. *Okay, God, I will take this step. But I make no promises. I'm not ready and You already know.*

Regardless of his intentions to treat this meeting as only a meeting and not a commitment to any further plans, he could no longer keep all this information from Jocelyn. He sent her a text, and they set up a time to meet on the next day she had off.

———

LAKE WAINSCOTT SHIMMERED in the midday sun as Jocelyn sat with Dylan on a bench beside the lake's walking and biking trails. After biking around to the north side of the lake, they'd stopped to eat lunch and now sat in contentment, enjoying the serenity that surrounded them. He wrapped his arm around her shoulders, and she tucked herself in closer. Sailboats, rowers, and kayakers took advantage of the beautiful sunny weather, despite the chill in the breeze.

Dylan toyed with the ends of her hair. "Would you like to go sailing sometime?"

Excitement bloomed in her chest. She hadn't gone in years. "I would love that."

"Have you heard anything more from the community hospital yet?"

"I submitted my application and test results. I talked to my HR contact at church, and she informed me the position they are looking to fill is a temporary one to fill in for someone going on maternity leave with an option to be hired full time afterward. But I haven't officially heard back from the hospital."

He rubbed his beard, gazing out over the lake. "Do you have another plan if the local hospital doesn't work out?"

She leaned into him, and he wrapped his arm more tightly around her. "To apply to the hospital in Walla Walla." She expelled a breath. Taking a position there would require a long commute, but the higher pay would be worth it.

"And a plan C?"

She laughed and covered her face. "Plan C is waiting for plan A and plan B to work. Oh, I take that back. Plan C is to get a roommate. That would help. But I really, really don't want to move away."

Dylan gathered her hands in his, kissed one, then turned and kissed her gently and tenderly. He rested a hand on her cheek. "I love you, and I'm proud of you."

Her eyes misted and her heart melted. She'd felt the same for some time and kissed him in lieu of a response.

But when she pulled away, something in his eyes indicated he wanted to say more.

"On New Year's Eve, you asked me if I'd tell you if I planned to return to Australia, and I promised to be open and honest with you."

Her heart sank, hard and fast. No! Tears formed in her eyes.

He held her fingers to his lips, then spoke again. "I'm not planning on going anywhere at the moment—but I do have a meeting with a missionary who is looking for someone to join him on a short-term mission trip."

"For how long?"

"Three to six months."

She blinked against the moisture in her eyes, and he gently wiped a stray tear.

"When?"

"I don't know yet."

"Are you planning on going?"

He shook his head and expelled a breath. "That's just it. I don't know what to do." He turned toward the water again, releasing her hands. He scrubbed his face, then glanced back at her with a sadness in his eyes that made her heart ache. "God is calling me back into the mission field, and frankly, I am terrified. That's why I haven't said anything." He gripped her hand again. "I don't want to leave you. I don't want to leave here. Not now, not when we've just begun. I don't understand why God is asking me to give up something I never thought I'd have again."

She'd never seen him wrestle with God like this. His spiritual demeanor always came across as steadfast and strong. She covered his hand and sat in patient silence while he continued.

"I've come to grips with Elise's death, yes, but to go back to the continent where she died? I don't think I can do that yet, and I certainly can't imagine taking someone else I love. Not again."

Her heart ached for him, for the wrenching decisions he had to make for himself. "Then why did you agree to the meeting?"

He leaned back, frowning, contemplative. "Because it requires no commitment right now. And maybe I could pass on the information I learn to another younger man who's interested in overseas missions." He rubbed his eyes. "Whether God allows this opportunity to be passed on to someone else ... who knows?"

She reached out a hand and turned his face toward her.

"Remember when you told me not to put my dreams on hold for you?" She cleared away the waver in her voice. "I love you enough to tell you the same thing."

He opened his mouth but didn't answer right away. The desperate sadness in his eyes revealed his tortured thoughts. "What if my dream is to be with you?" He leaned his forehead against hers, gripping her hand in his. "I can't imagine leaving you right now, Jocelyn."

She couldn't imagine him leaving either, but she also couldn't fathom holding him back from God's plan for his life. Even if that meant she'd not see him again for a long, long time.

CHAPTER TWENTY-FOUR

Dylan and Wyatt Stevenson, the Eternity Missions rep, listened together as the elderly pastor spoke from a quaint, sparsely furnished hut in a Ugandan village. The video flickered, froze, and refocused again. Wyatt sat beside Dylan and asked questions Dylan knew he should be asking himself.

Through their conversation, Dylan learned that Pastor Peter Brigham and his wife Doreen were directors of a rural primary school in Uganda, which was also attached to a church, and that they were seeking another director with both an educational background, and a strong pastoral and theological background. Dylan hadn't expected any of this, but it made sense, as educational facilities were favored in developing countries.

Still, he felt completely unqualified for this kind of position.

In a gap in the conversation, Dylan finally cleared his throat, prepared to ask his own questions. "What is your timeline for transferring director and pastoral duties over to another missionary?"

"Well, our timeline all depends on the next willing mission-ary's availability, but we're praying that we can transfer out within a year." The elderly pastor threaded his fingers through his wife's, who sat beside him.

Dylan held his head in his hand. This wasn't nearly so noncommittal a meeting as he'd been expecting. In his enthusiasm, Wyatt, someone he'd not worked with before, had assumed that Dylan agreeing to the meeting meant he had agreed to go overseas. Even Ethan had worn a giddiness in his expressiotn earlier that indicated cautious optimism, certainly more optimism than Dylan felt himself.

Thankfully, the Brighams appeared calmer and more level-headed.

Dylan muted the video briefly and turned toward Wyatt. "Can you excuse us a moment?' He gestured toward the video feed.

Wyatt's smile remained in place. "Sure." He stood, pushed in his chair, and left the room.

Dylan exhaled and unmuted the video. "I'm curious. What made you think of me, of all people? Sure, I've two long-term mission assignments under my belt, but the first was only a year in length, and the second one was tragically interrupted. I've had a limited educational background, which doesn't include working with children. So why me?"

Pastor Brigham and Doreen shared a contemplative glance, then he smiled a grandfatherly, compassionate smile back at Dylan. "We've heard a lot about you, and you do have experience in this region. You come highly recommended. Yes, we heard your story, and I know it happened years ago, but we extend our deep condolences. Know that we pray for you often."

He bowed his head. "Thank you." He'd heard of people he'd never met before praying over him while he grieved for so many years. Regardless of how long ago they may have been praying, the compassion in such acts touched the deepest recesses of his heart. This kindness truly reminded him of God's everlasting, watchful care over his life.

"Of course we want anyone interested to take time to prayerfully consider this," Doreen said. "But there is no pressure. We'd love to have you visit for a few months to see if this is truly a place and a position where you feel God would want you to minister."

"There is no long-term commitment," Pastor Brigham added. "Regardless of what anyone else is saying on your side." He chuckled. "We're constantly praying, and we are prepared to wait for the right person."

After more encouragement on their part, Dylan's profuse thanks for their understanding and patience, and a promise to speak again, he ended the video call.

He bowed his head to the table.

Short-term missions he could do. He could go for a few months and return. Recuperate. His last long-term trip had proven difficult for many reasons—being newly married, living in a remote village in a developing country. Yes, he'd returned home with heaps of wisdom, but he'd also returned in a state of devastation.

If he were honest, he and Elise should've waited. Maybe short-term missions were the way to go. He could evangelize, or in this case, minister to children in need, and maintain his growing relationship with Jocelyn.

But the choking fear remained, stealing his breath, and causing his heart to race.

"Lord God, if You truly want me to return, You're going to have to speak a little louder, because I don't know if I can do all of this again."

———

Jocelyn blinked hard at the name on the missed call and voicemail. Courtney, a name she hadn't seen in years. Why would Renee's sister call her? Sure, they'd been friends in high school and were still friends on social media, but they hadn't talked face-to-face since Dad's funeral. She expelled a breath and cautiously tapped the voicemail to listen.

"Hey, Jocelyn, this is Courtney Somers. How are you? I heard from Renee that you've finally graduated. Congratulations! That's exciting. I'm calling because I have it on good authority that you're looking for a nursing job. There are multiple immediate nursing openings here at Providence St. Mary's in Walla Walla. Anyway, thought I'd reach out at least. Call or message me anytime and I'll give you all the info you need to apply. Talk soon."

Jocelyn pursed her lips and listened again. Walla Walla wasn't that far. Applying there had been her second choice. The only major concern would be driving back and forth in the winter during snowfall.

Knowing someone who could put in a good word always helped when trying to get a job, and Courtney's call gave Jocelyn that introduction.

She finished stirring her pot of chicken noodle soup on the stove, poured a portion into a bowl, and brought the soup and her phone to the table. She should talk to Dylan about this. Or apply first, then talk to him?

What if he wanted to visit his family in Australia? She'd love to go with him, but she'd never be able to afford a round-trip flight on her current salary while paying over fifty percent of her paycheck toward the mortgage. She earned enough to survive, but hardly more than that.

Her heart yearned to remain in Trinity Lakes—to be with Dylan as much as to remain in the town where she'd grown up. But what if he chose to go overseas?

And what if my being here is holding him back from going overseas in the first place?

Long distance relationships didn't scare her. But did they scare him?

That evening, he called after she'd eaten dinner.

"You're off tomorrow, yes?" Dylan's voice came over the line, bringing her out of her internal debate.

"Yes."

"Let's go sailing?"

She grinned with anticipation, grateful for the distraction. "I would love that." Maybe tomorrow they could talk more.

———

AGAIN, Jocelyn blinked gritty eyes open at the sound of children crying. The same bright light surrounded her in the same tiny room. The same woman burst into the room in a wide-eyed frenzy, asked for help, then rushed off as abruptly as she'd appeared.

Jocelyn pushed herself up and followed the woman into a vast, open room filled with patients—African patients—being triaged by nurses of all nationalities. Some patients sat in chairs with children on their laps. Patients of all ages waited in lines which snaked out the door.

Curiosity tugged her feet forward toward the exit. Outside, she found herself in a village where makeshift buildings crowded the dusty streets. While the building she stood in was fashioned from colorfully painted stone, every other building nearby appeared ready to collapse in the next strong storm.

People clogged the dirt roads, some selling goods, some waiting in line for the medical clinic, others traveling back and forth.

The English woman appeared again and gestured for Jocelyn to follow. They wove through groups of people. The woman wore a stethoscope around her neck and took her place in line among the many others who were triaging patients.

She turned toward Jocelyn. "Are you a nurse?"

Jocelyn nodded, still at a loss for words.

'Good. You can help."

The thought that she should mention she'd only just received her licensing crossed her mind, but there wasn't time for clarification. Time flew by as she triaged patients next to the English woman. English, French, and languages she couldn't name blurred together in a cacophony as patients were sent here and there based upon their need. Daylight faded and blurred into night. Lamps, candles, and lanterns provided some light as the line thinned out.

Then Dylan appeared, dressed in a collared shirt and khaki shorts, his hair longer, his beard fuller. He knelt next to an African man in a wheelchair, held the man's hand, and bowed his head in prayer.

Tears welled in her eyes. After his prayer, he stood and grinned as he caught her eye. He closed the distance between them and captured both her hands in his.

"What are you doing here?" she asked.

He smiled that gentle, tender smile he held for only her. "I came to see you."

Jocelyn sat up with a gasp, her eyes wet. She ran her hands down her fuzzy pajama pants to reassure herself that she was indeed back in Trinity Lakes.

But that dream had felt *real*, so incredibly real. She could hear, see, touch, smell, and feel everything, including Dylan holding her hands. The expression of pure peace and joy on his face elicited more moisture in her eyes. He'd stood there, praying among the Africans, as if he belonged right there, and nowhere else.

Her heart ached with deep affection and engulfing sadness, and she curled forward into a ball on her bed. Jake's prediction had been right. Dylan's leaving was never a question of if, but of when. Whether Dylan traveled overseas for six months or six years, she had to let him go, no matter the cost.

CHAPTER TWENTY-FIVE

Dylan surveyed the shimmering lake from aboard a small sailing dingy. He wrapped his arm around Jocelyn, who sat beside him, while their sailing guide worked the sail in front.

Azure blue skies smattered with clouds to the east made this the perfect day to go sailing. With temperatures having warmed over Spring Break, multiple kayaks, canoes, and sailboats dotted the lake's surface.

The wind whipped through his hair and propelled the boat along the water while their guide deftly steered them clear of other boaters. Dylan was perfectly content to sit in silence and appreciate the ambiance of the lake around him instead of discussing anything to do with the looming decisions he had to make. He had too much on his mind to be a good conversationalist. Seemed Jocelyn felt the same way this morning as she leaned into him with a contented, quiet smile.

On top of avoiding the discussion of whether or not he should go overseas, he had another pressing matter to consider with a fast-approaching deadline he could no longer ignore.

When Ethan married in August, Dylan would need to either head back to Australia or find his own residence. Financially speaking, it would be difficult to find a place of his own to afford Trinity Lakes, unless it was in a shared roommate situation. Renting in a small somewhat isolated mountain town was no easy feat. Available rentals were limited and expensive and honestly, he didn't want to live in a one-bedroom rental.

It didn't escape his thoughts that some of these worries would be eliminated if he chose to go overseas.

Jocelyn bumped his shoulder, capturing his attention. "How did the video call go with the missionary pastor from Africa?"

He rubbed his beard. "All things considered, the conversation went well. The pastor and his wife are acting directors of a rural school in Uganda. They're fine missionaries and have assured me there is no pressure on my part."

"That's great, right?" She smiled and the sun glinted off her sunglasses.

"Well, if it weren't for the Eternity Missions rep's attitude, sure." He shrugged. Nothing to be done about that, as he couldn't change the man's job title and role in this whole thing. He would have to trust the pastor's word. Dylan would be the one to make the decision to stay or go. No one else.

"What do you mean by that?"

He expelled a heavy breath. "The mission organization is pressing for me to go, as I've partnered with them before on short-term and long-term missions, and I know the region." He scrubbed his face.

"But you don't want to go?"

He shook his head. "I don't know what I want."

The boat slowed, the wind dying down for the moment. They moved across the gorgeous blue surface of the lake at a leisurely pace. Birds flew above their heads, while kayakers glided by on the right.

Dylan turned toward Jocelyn and captured both of her hands in his. "Actually, I do know what I want. I want nothing but you, Jocelyn."

"What if I told you I had a job offer from a hospital in Walla Walla?"

His heart knocked harder in his chest as he studied her steady gaze. This didn't sound like wishful thinking or hypothetical on her part. "Are you serious?"

She nodded. The reflection of the surface of the lake shone in her brown lenses. "Would that impact your decision to take this mission opportunity?"

"Would you be commuting or moving away altogether?"

She glanced away, studying a small flock of ducks that had congregated near the shoreline. "I don't know."

"What about the local job offer you'd talked about?"

"The offered position in Trinity Lakes is temporary, and I won't know for sure for another month. Providence St. Mary's is hiring full time nurses." She still wouldn't look at him.

"Jocelyn." He perched his sunglasses on his head and rubbed his eyes, struggling to control the rising panic. Why did she want to leave? "If you're only pursuing this job to compel me to go overseas—"

She finally turned toward him, her gaze steady and firm. "I'm not afraid of a long-distance relationship, Dylan."

He opened his mouth with the intention to object but closed it again. She wasn't, sure, but he was downright terrified.

Her expression changed into something less tortured. She lifted her sunglasses to her head. "I have to tell you something else."

What? Tell him what? What was this unusual expression of sadness mixed with wonder?

While they floated around the lake, she told him of a strange dream she'd been having, where she woke up alone to the sound of children crying, and an English doctor would come into her room to ask if she had come to help.

"It's the same every time?"

She nodded.

"Why didn't you tell me about this sooner?"

She shrugged. "The dream was short and always ended abruptly—until last night." She gripped his hands tighter. "Last night was the first time the dream extended beyond a woman asking me for help before disappearing."

She recounted the rest of the dream, of how she found herself working as a medical missionary in Africa, and how, at the end of her dream, she'd seen him among the crowd, praying with others.

When she finished, he could hardly breathe. He framed her beautiful face with his hands. This was too good to be true. Had to be. How could it possibly be true?

"Dylan?"

"You saw me?" His voice rasped and he cleared the emotion away.

She nodded, that wonder returning, pronounced in her widening eyes. "And I have never seen you look more at peace."

Could this mean they were meant to go overseas together? But the process of applying for and raising funding for medical mission programs could take a year—assuming there were no hiccups. And the chances of them being sent together were slim to none, especially if they weren't working under the same sending organization. Unless …

No. He couldn't scare her like that. Even if everything in him wanted to bend down on one knee right here in the middle of the lake.

Not yet.

The firm voice of God descended, like a warm hand on his chest, a gentle reminder to be patient. *But what is this dream if not a divine vision of the future?*

Of course, he was being presumptuous. He'd heard numerous stories of other missionaries. Some were called young and didn't go into missions until ten or fifteen years later. Others never felt the call until they were in the field during some short-term trip. Others still, who weren't called until they were middle aged or older. God's plans were as vast as the number of missionaries around the world. No one could predict or understand God's timing except the Almighty Himself.

Dylan's hands moved to her hands again. His heart pounded. "What do you think the dream means for you?"

"I don't know what it means for me. I love helping people, I love my job, but I've only just graduated." She blinked rapidly and wiped a tear from beneath her eye. "The moment I saw you standing there in my dream, I knew that is where you're meant to be."

He ran a hand along her face again, fingering her hair. "What if He's calling you too?"

She blinked watery eyes. "I'm far from ready for anything like that."

"You don't have to be ready, Jocelyn. All you have to do is be willing."

CHAPTER TWENTY-SIX

A week after Easter, Jocelyn met Dylan in the church foyer before service. He grinned that familiar, intense grin that made her giddy inside. Ever since he'd begun attending church with her in January, Sunday had become her favorite day of the week. She'd managed to keep most Sundays off, which meant they often dedicated the entire day to each other. Today would be no different, she was sure.

Instead of dropping a kiss on her cheek as he sometimes did, he captured her hand in his as they navigated the influx of churchgoers entering the building. Before entering the sanctuary, he tugged her toward a more private alcove where the volume of conversation wasn't so loud, then turned to face her. "Ethan invited me to dinner tonight with his family, but I'd rather spend time with you."

She pursed her lips, the temptation to invite herself on the tip of her tongue.

He smiled gently. "I'd invite you if it were just Ethan and Lillian, but these are my former in-laws. Lillian's future in-laws. Frankly, it would feel odd."

"I totally get that." She'd likely feel out of place as well.

"Can I take you out tonight? Somewhere nice?"

She bounced on her toes. "I would love that."

"And lunch too? Downtown?"

She giggled. "My only plans are to be with you all day."

He dropped a kiss to her cheek then led her back into the foyer toward the sanctuary.

They found seats together. After the singing finished, and when the sermon began, Dylan captured her hand and held it in his lap, as if he were afraid she would stand and walk away.

As Pastor Ladan spoke on God's request to Abraham to sacrifice his son, she tuned out the story she'd heard plenty as a kid.

Her mind whirled with all the unknowns. They'd not talked about her dream since their sailing trip, nor had they discussed her tentative job opportunity in Walla Walla. Dylan seemed to be avoiding all the difficult conversations. But deep down, she knew the conversation regarding each of their futures was far from over.

He'd said she needed to be willing to answer any kind of call God had, but was he willing? What if he chose to stay and ignore his call because of her? Or what if he chose to stay for his own personal reasons? The only way she'd know, is if she accepted a job out of the city. Anyway, what would it hurt to apply? Spring was in full swing now, and she would have plenty of time to figure out what to do before next winter.

Then Pastor Ladan's words caught her attention. "Maybe today you are on the precipice of taking a leap of faith you can't fathom working out for your benefit. But God, in His infinite wisdom, always works everything for your good. Always."

Out of the corner of her eye, Jocelyn could see Dylan's expression changing.

"Let's talk about that word, faith. Hebrews eleven says, 'Faith shows the reality of what we hope for; it is the evidence of things we cannot see. By faith we understand that the entire universe was formed at God's command, that what we now see did not come from anything that can be seen.' Hebrews goes on to list biblical figures who displayed strong faith, Abraham being one."

Dylan's relaxed demeanor from earlier drained away, and he sat with rapt attention, listening as Pastor Ladan continued.

"Folks, Abraham displayed two attitudes I think are vital in our walk with God, both related to the attitude of willingness. Abraham was willing to sacrifice—throughout his entire walk with God, in fact—but in this one moment, he was willing to sacrifice something he loved. He was also willing to trust God because he had already seen God's care over his lifetime."

The message was hitting Dylan hard.

After Pastor Ladan concluded his sermon with a prayer, they fell in step together as they exited along with the rest of the congregation.

Dylan's hand found hers while they walked. "Shall we go for a walk along the river?"

That Dylan didn't want to eat lunch right away didn't surprise Jocelyn. She agreed, and they chose to leave the car and walk toward the water.

Her stomach clenched and the conversation they'd had while sailing surfaced again. *Not if, but when.* She expelled a heavy breath, asking God for strength in that moment, whenever it came, whether they discussed Dylan's future now or later. She couldn't do this alone.

DYLAN'S HEAD spun with the clear and present decision he had to make staring him in the face. God was again testing his willingness to sacrifice everything he'd come to love.

Well, God had certainly answered Dylan's prayers. If that

sermon wasn't God shouting at him, he sure didn't know what else to make of it.

And maybe, if he were honest, God had been shouting at him earlier than today. Like when Jocelyn had told him about her dream, about how she had seen him in Africa again.

He walked in silence alongside Jocelyn, hands in his coat pockets. They approached the riverbank skirted on both sides by pines, with hills and mountain peaks as their backdrop.

He focused on the mountains to the northeast, but a completely different mountain formed in his mind. How incredibly humbled and exhilarated and terrified Moses must have been while standing on Mount Sinai, listening to the majestic voice of the One who formed all things! All of the biblical figures who had heard God's voice on a mountaintop filtered through his mind.

Mountaintops were places of great transformation. One had been for him—for them both—back in November.

He cut a sideways glance toward Jocelyn. *Lord, if You are the one who crafts and designs all destinies and guides all our paths, why did You bring us together only to have me leave again?*

Jocelyn's eyes filled with tears. "You have to go, don't you?"

Those tears would be his undoing. He shook his head. "I don't have to do anything."

She folded her arms tight, but her gaze never left his.

He shook his head again and focused on the water. He'd take her hand and pull her into his arms if they weren't tucked close against her body. "I love you. I don't want to leave you. Nor do I want to bring you along." He closed the distance between them and held a hand to her face, letting her hair fall over his hand. "I can't go through losing someone else I love so dearly. Not again."

"Dylan, you could lose me any day of the week." She wiped at a stray tear on her cheek.

He choked on a ball of rising emotion. Dropping his hand,

he stepped away and focused on the current of the river. "Don't say that."

"Besides, this isn't about you and me. This is only about you." She moved to stand in front of him and captured both his hands in hers. "This is a call on your life. A call you alone need to answer."

"But—"

She shook her head this time. "I know you loved Elise, and I know you love me. I see it in every action you do. I love you too." She paused a moment, blinking against her tears. "But please don't let me be the reason you aren't following the path God has directed for you. That could be detrimental to both of us in the long run."

Deep affection welled from within, causing the back of his eyes to burn. She was too good to be true. God had truly blessed him, though he didn't feel he deserved any of it.

Capturing a kiss didn't even begin to seem a sufficient way to express how much he loved and adored her. How could this woman, someone he'd only known since November, love him enough to send him off like this? How could she know those words were everything he needed to hear and everything he'd prayed for?

When they broke apart, she bent her forehead to his. "Don't worry about me. I'll be right here, waiting."

He chuckled and kissed her again. "You act like I'm leaving for the airport right now. I'll tell you, I'm not yet." He tangled his hands in her hair. "How am I so blessed to be part of your life?"

She kissed him this time, and the aching sadness that had gripped him the moment the message registered in his soul this morning gradually morphed into joy.

But tears still ran down her cheeks. He wiped them away with his thumbs and pushed hair out of her face. "Come on, now. Let's not spend the rest of the day worrying about me leaving. I have a surprise for you later, and I can't have you all teary-eyed."

She smiled and stepped back, wiping her face with the sleeves of her jacket. "What surprise do you have for me?"

He smiled now, captured her hand, and together they walked to her car. "I thought we could call my family in Australia later and introduce you."

She gasped and brightened, her eyes sparkling. "I would love that."

They joined the typical Sunday crowd at Joe's Diner and waited to order. With the weather warming and lake tourism increasing, the diner had set up outside patio furniture to accommodate the extra patrons.

One of Jocelyn's acquaintances who attended regularly, nodded toward them as he and Jocelyn sat outside together, waiting for their orders. He approached them with an amiable smile.

"This is going to sound crazy, since you're a professor and all …" He cleared his throat and his expression turned sheepish and shy. "I'm helping lead a church bible study on Friday nights for young adults. Would you two be interested?"

Jocelyn smiled and nodded. "When I'm not working, sure."

Dylan nodded and reached for Jocelyn's hand. "That sounds like a great idea."

In fact, it was almost as if it were another answer to prayer, one he hadn't known he'd needed to pray.

CHAPTER TWENTY-SEVEN

Jocelyn smiled into Dylan's phone camera as Dylan's family came into view. Outside the cafe, streetlights flickered on along Main Street. But in Sydney, the sun shone through the living room window onto four adults seated on a navy-blue couch.

Everyone on the other side wore bright smiles and seemed to talk all at once, vying for a spot in front of the camera.

"Hi, Dylan!"

"Oh, he's got a girl with him."

"Who are you with, Dylan?"

"Shh, he already told us, remember?"

"Come on. Introduce us."

Dylan and Jocelyn laughed together. He entwined his fingers with hers as he introduced her. "Mum, this is my girlfriend, Jocelyn Monroe."

She politely waved hello. "Hi." Jocelyn's heart melted as the three women on the other side burst into excited conversation, talking over one another.

Dylan propped the phone up on the tabletop and then leaned back into the corner of the couch, wrapping an arm around Jocelyn so she could be in the line of the camera shot. "Jocelyn, this is my mum and dad, Adeline and Darwin, and my two youngest sisters, Lara and Maddy. Lara just began attending university last fall, and Maddy's set to attend this coming fall, yeah?" Maddy nodded with a shy grin.

They each introduced themselves in more detail, then they peppered Jocelyn with more questions, which she happily answered.

"How in the world did you two meet?" Maddy asked, her young eyes sparkling with romantic curiosity.

Jocelyn exchanged a glance with Dylan, who grinned, but remained mute on the subject. Fine. She'd tell the story from her point of view.

"Well, as I mentioned, I'm a paramedic, and I also volunteer with the ski patrol. Over Thanksgiving break, Dylan got stuck near the top of a ski run, and I had to rescue him because I thought he might have a concussion—"

"—I'd like to add that I was completely fine."

The girls both giggled. Jocelyn cast a glance sideways. "You were not fine. I wasn't about to let a dizzy man ski down the hill alone only for him to fly into a tree."

Dylan's brows rose in mock offense. "I was not dizzy. I was completely level-headed."

Jocelyn rolled her eyes.

"So how did you get down the mountain then?" Maddy sat forward on the couch.

Dylan frowned and Jocelyn jumped to answer. "I had him ride on the back of my snowmobile."

The girls collapsed into more giggles.

"Is that allowed?" This from his mom.

"Not really."

Dylan shot a mock glare at her. "No?"

She grinned. Had she never mentioned that before?

His brows drew together. "You never told me about that."

"You never asked."

"I assumed you were following protocol." His forehead furrowed. "I didn't think there was anything to ask about regarding riding on a snowmobile with you."

The entire family laughed, drawing her attention back to the screen.

They spoke with his family for another half an hour, catching up on life and his and Jocelyn's relationship. After the call ended, they finished dinner, then Dylan dropped her home.

She relished his embrace and rested against his shoulder, her heart overflowing.

"Thank you for tonight. What a fun surprise."

He pressed a kiss into her hair. "I thought you would enjoy that."

"Your family seems wonderful."

"I like to think so." He chuckled. "So I didn't get you in trouble up at the ski resort?"

She laughed into his shoulder. "No."

"Promise?"

She pulled back and locked eyes with his. "Everything worked out."

He tilted his head with a skeptical expression, then stole a kiss. "I don't know if I believe you."

She laughed and leaned into his chest again.

His grin faded and his expression sobered. "Weren't you afraid of risking your position, pulling a stunt like that?"

She pursed her lips. Had she been? She shook her head. "To be honest, I was much more concerned about you. I know we're not supposed to force anyone to accept medical aid, but I was legitimately concerned about you skiing again while disoriented."

He bent his forehead to hers and closed his eyes. "Admirable, truly. Even if it went against protocol."

She rested her hands against his chest and focused on the strength of his heartbeat beneath her fingertips.

"Will you do a Bible study or devotion with me?" His hands roamed down her back. "We could text or call each day after we each read the daily chapters. I promise not to go too deep into theology and all that."

She rarely had the privilege of hearing him drop into theological discussions, but the prospect thrilled her. She pulled back and gazed upward. "I would love to."

"Perfect." He kissed her again. "I should say goodnight."

She smiled into another kiss. "Yeah, you should." But she could stand here all night with his arms around her, and the world would be perfect and right.

EVERY MOMENT JOCELYN spent with Dylan became even more precious now that he'd made tentative plans to go overseas. The evenings they couldn't see each other, they talked on the phone, going over the chapters they'd read that day.

Friday nights became her new favorite night of the week. Even after an exhausting day at work, she made it a priority to attend the church Bible study with Dylan. There, she reconnected with old friends, and had the opportunity to listen to Dylan speak words filled with immense wisdom and knowledge. She could hardly believe she hadn't seen this side of him. How had they not attended a Bible study together before now? Oh, how she'd been missing out. The more he spoke to the group, the more her heart knew—teaching others about the Bible and hope of Christ was exactly what Dylan was meant to do.

After their third Friday night Bible study meeting, she drove Dylan home. As she pulled up to the curb in front of his house, he turned toward her in the darkness. "Will you go on a walk with me?"

She smiled and nodded, eager for any kind of excuse to spend more time with him.

A cool wind blew through the trees as they ambled through the tranquil northside neighborhood streets located in between the Bible college and seminary campuses. Jocelyn zipped up her jacket, then Dylan captured her hand in his.

"You were amazing tonight. I wish sometimes I'd taken a class from you last semester." She grinned, reveling in the knowledge he possessed.

Dylan stopped, then turned toward her. "I don't."

She met his gaze in the dark but couldn't quite read his expression. He stood in front of her and captured her other hand. "A high level of professionalism is required from all teachers. There's a delicate balance of power that exists between student and teacher, and rightly so. Given how hard I fell for you in just one week, having you in a class would've proven detrimental to both of us." He wove his fingers in between hers. "I never want to think of you as another passing student. You are much more valuable than that."

He captured and held a long and tender kiss that left her breathless—she would never tire of that—then coaxed her to walk with him again.

Darkness surrounded them, until the moon broke through the clouds. They crested the top of a small hill and found the moon shining on the waters of the lake and river, and lights sparkling from the neighborhoods on Lake Wainscott's southern shore.

"I can't believe school is out in a month." Dylan still held her hand as they stared at the moon over the lake, its light shifting in and out of the clouds.

She turned toward him, a hint of panic rising within. *Lord, bring me peace.* After all, she'd encouraged him to pursue missions in spite of her. Panicking would get her nowhere.

He squeezed her hand as they walked. "I wanted to update you. I have a meeting coming up with the missionary pastor and his wife to talk about the specifics of traveling to serve with them."

She pushed back against the fear of the unknown. Dylan needed to take this step. He needed to walk in faith and face his fears and he needed her unwavering support. "Do you know when you would be leaving?"

He shook his head. "That's what I aim to find out. I don't know anything for sure, but I'm expecting I can finish teaching this semester at least. It takes time to organize travel and obtain visas and everything."

He gently coaxed her to follow him back toward her car. When they reached her car, he leaned against the hood and pulled her into his arms. She buried her face in his chest, relishing the safety and warmth of his arms. Safety she hadn't felt in years, not since before she'd left home, before she'd entered into a dead-end relationship, before her parents had split.

He caressed the top of her head. "No matter what happens, no matter how long I'm here for, or how long I'm gone, I love you."

"I love you too."

This was home. He was home.

Lord, bring him back to me, and help me be strong in his absence, so we can do the work You have planned for our lives together, whatever work that might be. And help me to prepare to do whatever You would have of me.

DYLAN EXPELLED a slow breath as he prepared to log into the video chat with Pastor Brigham. He'd spent the majority of today alone in one of the campus gardens, praying, reflecting, and reaffirming his decision to take this opportunity. *God, Your will be done.*

As before, Peter and Doreen were pleasant, easygoing, and full of wisdom and life experience. They asked questions, and Dylan answered them with honest sincerity. He still didn't feel qualified or worthy of this opportunity, but both appeared joyful at his decision to join them on a short-term trip.

Afterward, they laid out a preliminary timeframe, and a list of recommended steps for him to take in order to prepare to travel. Eternity Missions would be the primary resource and guide for making everything happen, of course, but it helped to have a refresher on all the things that needed to be done in such a short time.

When their conversation ended, Dylan scanned the list he'd made. His mind whirled with how incredibly soon they wanted him to come, and all the things that had to be done first. He typically preferred to take time to process and plan things out.

Well, to be fair, he'd had time to process this, but he'd chosen to run in the opposite direction for a while.

Still. June? That was only six weeks away!

The front door opened, and Ethan entered, speaking on his phone as he walked through the house and down the hall. After ending his call, he emerged from the hall and entered the kitchen. "Hey, are you still interested in a used car? I've got a friend whose parents are selling their car."

He shook his head. "I won't need one."

Ethan pocketed his phone and stared at him with a furrowed brow. "Is it the cost? Didn't you mention you had money saved up? I could always split the cost with you."

"I might not need it." Dylan smiled and shook his head again. "I'm going to Uganda in June."

CHAPTER TWENTY-EIGHT

"Did I hear you right? He's leaving?" Jake's voice floated over the video feed in a high-pitched tone.

Jocelyn sat forward with her chin resting in her hand. "You predicted it would happen, remember? So why do you look so shocked?"

Jake leaned back against his faded leather couch and rubbed the back of his head. "I'm sorry I was a jerk for saying that. And I'm sorry he's leaving. I just didn't want to see you get hurt again ... Wait. You seem suspiciously calm about this whole thing." His brow furrowed. "Why aren't you crying or something?'

Jocelyn couldn't fight the laugh that burst through. Despite the looming date of Dylan's departure, peace encased her heart like protective armor. Some nights she succumbed to the sadness and cried, then she prayed God's protection over Dylan until she fell asleep. Most days, she simply enjoyed every single moment they had together.

"He's going on a short-term mission trip to Africa. He'll be back."

Jake sat forward. "Oh. Not back to Australia?"

"Maybe someday." She smiled again. They'd talked to his family together at least once a week since April and he'd told them about his plans for travel to Africa again, to mixed reactions. She'd told them about her dream, of how she'd seen him in Africa, and how completely at peace he'd appeared. That alleviated some of their unease. Even if it was only a dream.

But what if it wasn't just a dream? What if God was calling her into missions as well? She'd kept the thought far back in her mind, but Dylan spoke of it often. He'd told her stories of people who had been called to missions very young, but weren't ready for twenty years.

Regardless of where God called Dylan overseas, the more she became entangled in his life, the more she knew she wanted to visit Australia with him, whenever that may be. She needed to put her degree to use and learn the valuable skills that, someday, she might use overseas. She'd not be able to use those skills overseas if she didn't get an actual job in nursing.

In the beginning of May, she'd finally contacted Courtney, then filled out the application for the nursing position at Providence St. Mary's. Last week, both Trinity Lakes Community Hospital *and* Providence St. Mary's had contacted her to set up interviews. Now, she needed to decide whether to take a local temporary position, or a full time position out of town. Regardless, she'd finally be earning enough money to travel.

Wouldn't it be amazing to spend Christmas in Australia with Dylan? Though she loved winters here, visiting Australia for a summer Christmas sounded fantastic. Of course, they would visit his family, and they could even go to the beach and swim!

"I haven't seen you smile like that in years."

She blinked and found Jake staring hard at her.

"You really love him, don't you?"

Affection swelled within her heart. "More than I thought possible."

"You're not upset that he's leaving?"

"I'm a little sad, yes." She lifted her shoulder. "But I fully believe this is what God has called him to do, and I trust that God will bring us back together."

A deep frown disturbed Jake's scruffy face. He cleared his throat and leaned backward again. "I've got somewhere to be in a little while, so I should—"

Jocelyn sat forward. "Wait, I got sidetracked. I actually called you for a different reason."

Jake sat silent, waiting.

"Remember how I asked if you wanted to come back to Trinity Lakes?"

He frowned, but she recognized his expression of deep contemplation. Good. That meant he'd kept his promise to at least think about the idea.

"I could still use a roommate."

"I'd have to find a job first, to be able to contribute to rent and all." He folded his arms. "Are jobs still as scarce there as they were six-ish years ago?"

"If I can help find you a job here, will you move back and room with me?"

Jake continued to frown, but she could see those wheels turning. Finally, he nodded.

She released a giddy breath of excitement. "Yes!"

Jake scowled and his eyes narrowed, as if he regretted speaking so soon. "Joss..."

She lay backwards down on the couch, still laughing. She didn't care if that nod indicated more of a "maybe" than a "yes". That he wanted to come back at all was a win, and her heart overflowed with a burst of exhilarating anticipation. Wait until she told Dylan.

"Don't get so excited. I haven't hopped on a plane just yet."

She sat back up and grinned.

"I'm serious. I'm not moving anywhere without a job lined up."

She rolled her eyes and shook her head. "All right. We'll figure that out together."

————

Their time was up.

Today he walked by faith. Rather, leapt by faith into the unknown. It felt akin to jumping off a cliff, praying the parachute you'd packed worked correctly. Or zip-lining. Well, at least he'd accomplished zip-lining.

Dawn painted the sky in vibrant pink and orange and lavender and gradually lit the dim kitchen where Dylan sat. He rubbed weary eyes and sipped his second cup of coffee, made stronger than usual. Instead of nightmares waking him, last night he'd hardly slept because of the pile of unknowns weighing down his stomach.

The last month had flown by in a single breath. All the tasks he needed to complete before traveling overseas were double-checked and done and he'd set all his finances to autopay. Because of his looming departure, he made every effort to spend every day with Jocelyn. If they couldn't see each other, they talked on the phone. Each moment with her felt like a blessing, and he stored the memories in his heart to call upon during his lengthy absence.

Knowing she now had a secure higher-paying nursing position eased some of his concerns over her future, even though she worked in Walla Walla. So far, she loved her team, and he'd been thrilled when she'd mentioned saving up to visit Australia later in the year. He had no doubt she was right where she needed to be. Whether she used her skills to work overseas or remained Stateside, God had plans for her, and he could not wait to walk beside her through that journey.

Despite his preparedness, the reality of his departure sat

heavy as an anvil on his chest as he stared at the packed bags spread on the couch in the living room.

Birdsong drifted through the window. He should get going if he wanted to make the most of this last day with Jocelyn. He gathered his belongings into a backpack. Journal, Bible, phone, tablet, chargers, keys, wallet, water bottles.

Ethan appeared in the kitchen wearing a t-shirt and shorts, hair sticking up all over his head. "You're up early."

"So are you, mate." Sometimes Dylan swore this guy could function on an hour of sleep.

Ethan set a folded piece of paper on the counter. Dylan frowned and eyed the familiar worn edges.

Ethan eyed him. "You said you'd read this before my wedding."

He inhaled a deep breath. Ethan was giving him this letter now?

"I can't take that with me. What if I lose it?" Two months was a long time away.

He folded his arms. "Then you should read it sooner rather than later."

Dylan blinked and rubbed his eyes again. He couldn't do this now. Not when his emotions were already frayed over leaving the woman he loved. "Why didn't you wait to give it to me later, before I leave tonight?"

Ethan didn't answer. Dylan raked his fingers through his hair.

"Please, Dylan." Ethan leaned against the counter. "You said you'd read it. For me."

Blast it all. Ethan's wavering tone indicated he was as emotional as Dylan. He still didn't understand why the words in this letter were so important, but Ethan wouldn't have kept the piece of paper this long if they weren't.

"Fine." Dylan carefully placed the letter in between the pages of his Bible.

Ethan wandered to the coffee pot, emptied out the dregs and rinsed the pot to use for himself. "What time are you coming back today?"

"We'll drop by here after lunch."

After filling the pot with coffee grounds and water and setting it to brew, he turned toward Dylan with his character-istic cheerful smile. "Have the best day ever."

"Thanks. I plan to."

———

JOCELYN'S STOMACH TWISTED. Was she nervous or getting sick? Ugh, might be the anticipation of Dylan actually leaving on a plane today finally catching up to her.

Either way, she had no appetite this morning. But she forced down a piece of toast anyway—she'd be lightheaded if she skipped breakfast altogether. Good thing she'd taken today and tomorrow off.

He's leaving tonight. With no return flight planned. Stepping out in faith, into a shaky world where power and internet or even personal safety weren't guaranteed, and where children needed to know and see and hear the love of Jesus.

She blinked back the tears that kept popping up. She would not cry. Not yet, not until after she returned from the airport. Alone.

A knock on the door startled her from her morning devo-tion. She lifted her second cup of coffee and went to answer it, grateful she'd at least gotten dressed. Who was knocking on her door so early?

A misty haze covered the ground outside her window, and an unfamiliar car sat parked in front of her lawn. She opened the door to find Dylan standing with a gentle, tender smile.

She fell into his arms, still holding tears back. "What are you doing here so early?"

He held her close and caressed the top of her head. "I came to see you. I have a surprise for you."

She pulled him inside, then shared a long and tender kiss that she never wanted to end. Wisely, he broke apart and pressed one last kiss to the top of her hair. "Remember back in November, when we weren't sure if we'd see each other again and the future seemed so unclear?"

She nodded, her vision blurring.

"Remember I asked you to dinner and took you on a gondola ride?"

A tear tracked down her cheek, and then another.

"How about another gondola ride before I leave? What do you think, hm?"

More tears fell and he wiped them all away one by one. She could do no more than nod.

Once she had dressed more warmly and they'd packed a backpack with water and food to last them through lunch, he led her out to the unfamiliar car parked in front of her house.

"Whose is this?" She beamed as he stood smiling next to the driver's side door.

"Ethan gifted it to me yesterday after I came home. Even though I know he's using it as an incentive to get me to come back to Trinity Lakes in time for his wedding, I couldn't say no. I'm sure it'll come in handy."

Jocelyn laughed and climbed into the passenger seat. If he came back, she was sure it would be for far more than just a car.

———

AT THE RESORT, Dylan rented a pair of quad bikes, and they spent an hour rumbling along trails through beautiful dark green woodlands, saturated with the scent of pine and spruce. What a contrast to the pristine winter wonderland they'd first snowmobiled through together.

Afterward, they spent the rest of the morning hiking through the park. Wildflowers bloomed in abundance, carpeting the meadows and open spaces in between thickets of deep evergreens. They crested the top of a hill and stopped amid an open grassy meadow, resplendent in yellow, green, white, and lavender flowers. The perfect place to rest and eat.

From here they could see the gondola where he'd first kissed her glide across the park from the top of the mountain down to the bottom lodge. To the southwest, through a break in the sea of evergreen, Lake Wainscott glistened in the sun under a blue sky. The weather had warmed enough in the meadow to allow them to shed their coats. Dylan spread them on the ground so they had a place to eat lunch.

Once they'd settled with water and food in front of them, Dylan turned his focus to Jocelyn. "I have some news." He inhaled, steeling himself for the disappointment that was sure to follow with what he had to say. But after talking things over with Ethan last night, he concluded this was the best decision, for his own sanity.

"What's up?" She set down her bottle of water and picked up a chicken wrap.

He plunged forward. "Ethan's driving me to the airport tonight."

Her joyful and relaxed demeanor fell. *Lord, please help her understand.* She stared at the glimpse of the blue water in between the trees. "Why?"

He reached for her hand and brought the tips of her fingers to his lips. "If you drop me off Jocelyn, I don't trust myself to get on that plane."

She turned toward him with watery eyes. Food forgotten, he gently tugged her into his lap. The backs of his eyes burned even now, and he still had nearly twelve hours until his flight left. How could he leave her? This strong, determined, independent, and fearless woman whose greatest passion in life was to help the injured and save lives. This beautiful blessing from God, who had renewed the joy and life inside of him, something he'd thought he'd lost the day Elise died. Yes, he wanted to follow God, and yes, he wanted to put God first, but this was so hard.

God, please, bring me back to her.

After finishing lunch, they hiked back down toward the lodge, and then headed toward the gondola.

Riding the gondola was as magical and intimate as it had been on that wintery night months back. Miles and miles of beautiful green wilderness stretched below them, bordered by the town and its three glistening blue lakes. A shimmering river flowed west into rolling ranchland beyond that. A breathtaking view he'd not soon forget.

He wrapped Jocelyn in his arms and stifled the familiar compulsion to propose. He had been contemplating the idea for weeks, but God kept telling him to wait. So he would wait, until their future was more certain.

"This view is as beautiful as always." She leaned into his chest, with her gaze fixed out the huge window.

But he no longer studied the view out the window. Instead, he could do nothing more than study the outline of her face, if only to memorize it. Uncertainty and panic mixed with euphoria tugged on his heart, just as it had during their first ride together in November. This time, however, he chose to put his trust fully in God, something he should've done months and months ago when it came to this woman.

Gradually, the uncertainty ebbed away, leaving joy and love and affection. He ran a hand through her hair, twining a lock around his fingers. "I love you, Jocelyn," he whispered before capturing her mouth in his. He broke the kiss and pressed his forehead to hers while he caught his breath. "No matter how far I go."

"No matter how far you go," she murmured. "I love you too."

CHAPTER TWENTY-NINE

Light rain smattered against the rooftop of Dylan's small bungalow, the sound both soothing and heartbreaking. This was reminiscent of weather that had often brought him and Elise together while they lived and worked in Uganda years ago. The circulating memories of newly married life with Elise were tainted by the recollection of the heavy rains that had contributed to their car accident.

I shouldn't have brought Elise along. We should've waited.

He'd dissected this guilt for years through therapy. Logically, he knew the weather couldn't be controlled. Nor could the speed of oncoming drivers. None of these things were his fault, and neither was her death. But if he'd not convinced her to come with him ...

He'd dissected that argument over the years as well. Elise had been equally exuberant about preaching the gospel and global missions. He wouldn't have been able to stop her from joining him. In fact, she would love this little school and church where Dylan now assisted.

Even after years of dismantling all these arguments, those

old feelings of guilt reared up again. *How can I put another woman I love in danger again? And what of any future children?*

He lay on the bed, staring at the ceiling, Jocelyn's beautiful face smiling in his mind's eye. If anyone could handle herself in a dangerous country, it was Jocelyn Monroe. Brave, athletic, adventurous, intelligent, and skilled in all things survival and medical, she would be fine.

That thought brought him less comfort than he'd hoped.

He turned on his side and spied his open Bible, with the letter from Elise lying between the pages. The letter he'd attempted—and failed—to read multiple times since he'd arrived. Maybe her last words would alleviate some of his lingering guilt. Elise had exuded kindness and compassion from deep in her soul. She'd never, ever have blamed him, and she'd not want guilt to stagnate in his heart.

He sat up, opened the letter, but found his hands trembling. Confounded fear.

Why am I so afraid of words on a page from over four years ago?

He set the letter aside, found his phone and opened his world clock app to calculate the time difference between Uganda and Washington state. He sent a video call request to Jocelyn.

Jocelyn's smile and bright eyes warmed his heart. "Hey, handsome."

"Good morning, beautiful." He grinned into the camera, gratefulness expanding within. "I miss you."

"I miss you too." She blinked, studying him more carefully. "Everything okay?"

He eyed her nursing scrubs. Looked like she was walking down one of the hospital corridors. "I'm sorry for interrupting your day. I don't want to get you in trouble."

"I'm okay. I was just about to grab a snack. I can talk for a bit."

"Can you do me a favor?"

Her gentle smile remained, steadfast and unfaltering. "Of course. Anything."

He retrieved the letter from the middle of his Bible. "Ethan gave me a letter Elise wrote to him before she passed away. He made me promise to read it before his wedding."

She nodded, positioning herself closer to the camera.

"Frankly, I'm having a hard time with this." He rubbed his eyes and swallowed a burning lump in his throat.

"Why are you having a difficult time?" Her quiet and gentle tone held no accusation.

"Whatever she had to say must've been important, or Ethan wouldn't have kept it."

Jocelyn lifted a shoulder in an almost imperceptible shrug. "They're precious because they're the last words he read, sure, but they could also be completely ordinary words."

He blinked, contemplating her assessment. Had he been overcomplicating things for weeks? Building up the situation to be bigger than it was?

He cleared his throat and fingered the edges of the paper.

"It's all right, Dylan." Jocelyn's voice brought his eyes back to the screen.

With a deep inhale, he unfolded the letter and skimmed the first few lines, which he'd managed to read before. But, as always, he got stuck. Then, with Jocelyn's caring smile bolstering his courage, he began to read the rest.

Most of the letter contained updates on what they'd been accomplishing in their ministry. Then he stumbled upon a paragraph in the middle that stole his breath.

I know you're not big into making life-long promises, but will you promise me something? Will you look after Dylan if something happens to me? I just have this awful feeling in my stomach. Not fear exactly. Just a feeling. I know this sounds like crazy talk and honestly, either one of us could die in this dangerous area we work in.

If I don't come home, don't lose heart. Don't give up on yourself or

Dylan. Since the day we became engaged, I've prayed daily for God's protection and hand on both of us, but also that He would surround Dylan, because this line of work is intense.

I trust God's plan, no matter what happens. Will you pray with me for the two of us?

The words blurred together to where he could no longer decipher them, and Dylan found his cheeks wet with tears.

"Dylan?" Jocelyn's concerned tone brought him back to the video, just in time to watch it flicker. He tried to click and refresh the video feed, but it flickered again, and then shut off completely, the connection lost.

He heaved a heavy breath laden with emotion and wiped his face. Elise had known. But how? Was it the intensity of the Ugandan environment? Or had God truly warned her somehow? The idea would seem completely crazy to most people, but Dylan and Elise had been steadfast in their prayer life together. In a place without contact from a strong faith community, prayer had been paramount for both of them.

He didn't doubt her words. At the same time, he was grateful she'd never mentioned any such feelings to him. If he'd suspected she had any ill feelings about being in Uganda with him, he'd have whisked her back to Australia or the States in a heartbeat.

Maybe she'd never mentioned anything because she knew he needed to be there. Here. She knew these people needed to hear and see the love of Jesus firsthand, amid the difficult environment surrounding them.

Just one more reason he'd loved her so much. She always put others before herself.

Overwhelming affection caused the back of his eyes to burn again. Elise and Jocelyn each held plenty of differences, but both women had the same beautiful spirit overflowing with generosity and compassion toward others.

Elise might be gone now, but Jocelyn was alive and well, and courageous, generous and encouraging, waiting for him to come home.

———

AFTER WORK and the long drive home, Jocelyn wanted nothing more than to lounge on the couch in a comfy tank and pair of shorts. After she took a shower to wash off the heat and sweat of the day.

Gross. Ugh. Her house was so hot and stuffy.

She flipped on the air conditioner, then wavered in the hall. Should she shower or call Dylan first? What time was it there again? She didn't want to wake him up.

Helplessness had nearly overwhelmed her this morning when the video feed had cut out. That wasn't abnormal, as his internet connection was spotty at best. But to cut out right then, while he'd cried in the darkness, had brought tears to her own eyes. She'd had to stop and pray before going back to work.

Ten hours later, she was more than ready to see his face and make sure he was all right. She ignored the need for a shower and snagged her laptop in order to make the video call.

His smile was a welcome sight, and relief washed through her. "Good morning."

"Did you just get off work?" His eyes crinkled. Behind him, she could see a few local women scurrying around outside in the yard where he sat, possibly preparing a morning meal. Hard to tell from where he was positioned.

She ran a hand over her sweaty hair and leaned back onto the couch. "Is it that obvious?"

He chuckled, thankfully in a brighter mood than last night. "Well, your uniform is a dead giveaway."

She blinked back the tears of helplessness that threatened. "I wanted to make sure you were okay after last night."

That familiar gentle and tender smile she'd fallen in love

with illuminated his face. A smile she swore he wore for her and no one else in the world.

"I am much better. And thank you."

She pursed her lips and wiped the moisture clear from beneath her eyes. What had she done?

"You've always been brave, especially when I'm not. Thank you for being with me and encouraging me."

"Anytime." She ran her hand through her hair again. Ew. Sweaty. But she could wait.

"I have news for you." His smile brightened into a grin, and she reciprocated. "I just got off a call with Ethan. We finalized when I'll be flying in for his wedding."

She clapped her hands together and joy exploded within. "That's great! How long are you staying?"

"I've booked my flight for a week before, and a return flight for a week afterward."

A two-week stay! Best. News. Ever! Oh goodness, that desire to fold herself into his arms and revel in his warmth and strength caused her eyes to burn again. "I can't wait. I miss you so much."

"I miss you too, more than you can imagine."

CHAPTER THIRTY

Afternoon sun cast long golden rays of light over the tops of the trees that flanked the shoreline. Sailboats, canoes, and kayaks dotted the surface of Lake Wainscott, as did plenty of swimmers.

Jake's black lab, Zuzu, ran up and down the grass in front of where Jocelyn, Renee, and several other friends sat lounging on beach chairs in the sun.

Renee cast a glance in her direction, her sunglasses reflecting the shiny surface of the water. "Are you coming to my birthday dinner tonight?"

"Of course." Jocelyn stretched out her legs on the grass. "I'm stuffed from lunch, but I'll be there." She could eat something light. "But I need to drop my things home and shower first."

Renee nodded and fielded a text on her phone.

"Have you heard from Jesse lately?"

Renee shook her head, and a guarded expression crossed her face. "From all the mountain photos he's been posting on socials, he looks to be traveling a lot."

"Where to?"

She lifted a bare shoulder. "I've asked around and no one really knows anything."

Jocelyn pursed her lips and sipped from a water bottle. Jesse wasn't one to take off like this without notice. But he was also an experienced outdoorsman.

"Are your brother and sister in town?"

Renee nodded and her smile returned.

"That's great."

"I know. I haven't seen them in ages." Renee lifted her glasses and her grin morphed into something mischievous as she stared hard at Jocelyn. "Too bad Dylan couldn't be here."

Jocelyn's heart hiccupped. Oh, she missed him more than words could express. "One more week." Excitement bloomed in her chest.

"One more week!"

They both squealed like teenagers. Jocelyn didn't care how ridiculous she looked and sounded. A week from today, Dylan would land back in Washington, if only for a short time. She couldn't not count the minutes. This time, she would be at that airport.

By four, at the peak of the heat of the day, everyone began to pack up. Jocelyn could use the time to relax and shower, and maybe get Jake to help her clean the house a bit. With her long workdays and extra long commute from Walla Walla, she hardly had time to clean.

At least she could afford a gardener for the exterior, but the inside of the house had deteriorated significantly with the addition of another housemate and his dog. With how busy they both were, she couldn't figure out how everything became such a mess so quickly.

Jake approached the group, his dog loping behind him.

Renee stood up from stashing her belongings in her beach bag. "Are you coming tonight?"

He frowned, and his gaze skittered away. "I just found out about it. I've got things to handle at the restaurant."

Next to her, Renee lifted a shoulder, but Jocelyn frowned at him as she rolled her towel and found a place for it in her bag. "I thought you had the whole day off?"

Jake's gaze faltered again. "The restaurant can't open itself, you know. But happy birthday, Renee. Hope it's a fun night tonight."

"No big deal." Renee smiled at Jocelyn as she slung her beach bag over her shoulder. "See you at seven."

Jocelyn waved as Renee walked toward her car with a couple of other friends. A minute later, she fell in step next to Jake and Zuzu as they headed toward her car. She cut a sideways glare toward him. "You always do this."

"Do what?" His lips formed a firm line.

"You always run off." She studied him carefully, noting the crease in his forehead. She hoped this half day in the sun relaxing with friends had helped reduce his stress level.

He made a loud pfft sound. "I've already taken half the day off."

Okay. That she could understand. She opened her mouth to apologize, but Jake's tone changed.

"She's not even my friend. She's your friend. I'm not obligated to hang out with her or celebrate her birthday. We barely know each other. I have other people I hang out with."

He strode ahead of her toward her car. Zuzu followed dutifully behind, the long leash allowing for plenty of slack.

Once Jocelyn popped the trunk, Jake dumped his bag, chair, and towel haphazardly inside. "I'm riding with Justin." He threw his thumb toward the friends he'd been hanging with and turned in their direction. "I'll see you around."

What was his problem? She clenched her jaw and climbed into her car. She rolled down all the windows and flipped the AC to high. Sure, he was grumpy and stressed, but that didn't give him a right to be mean. They'd hung with Renee a couple of times since he'd returned, and the two seemed to get along fine. Unless Jake had faked it.

She should take a cold shower to wash off the irritation, but a bike ride sounded more appealing. She needed some serious exercise to get rid of this ire.

She rode her bike over the stone bridge and to the other side of the lake, then paused for a long drink of water and a rest. She checked the time. Oh! She'd need to head back if she wanted to have time to shower and change before heading to meet Renee.

A pang of loneliness and longing shot through her. She pushed the video chat option and sent a request to Dylan. She'd missed talking with him this morning because she'd slept in. When he didn't answer, she expelled a breath. Oh! It might be too early in the morning. Well then, she'd leave him a message and let him sleep.

"Good morning, handsome. I just called to say I miss you." She smiled brightly. "I can't wait to see you. Talk to you when you wake up."

She sent her recorded message, then stood and decided to stretch each leg a bit before heading back home on her bike. In the middle of stretching, her phone pinged.

Hey, beautiful. Everything all right?

She smiled as she typed.

I'm sorry if I woke you.

You're fine. What's going on? Tell me about your day.

She smiled again, drank the rest of her water bottle, and told him what all she'd done today and her plans for tonight. Then she vented a little about Jake.

Sorry to hear about Jake's attitude.

He sent a GIF of two people hugging.

Guys are complicated sometimes. I would know.

I miss you.

I miss you too. Don't worry about Jake. He's got a lot on his plate. Go. Have fun at the party.

Back at home, she took a quick, cold shower to wash away the irritation and sweat from being out in the sun all day, then dressed for dinner.

Parking along the lakefront down Main Street was at a premium this evening. How many people had Renee invited? Sure, tourism played a role in the higher-than-average population around town in July, but at seven at night, she should be able to find a parking spot near the Bellbird.

Parking three blocks down, she locked her car then back-tracked toward the café. As she approached, a crowd of people streamed from the restaurant's doors, cheering and clapping, some of them shouting "Surprise!" as they greeted her.

What in the world? Why were they shouting at her? She wasn't the person they were waiting for.

The more people she passed, the more faces she recognized. The Ladan family, plus Hallie Hollaway, all stood together smiling bright, with Brandon and Josie somewhere in the back of the group. Tabby from the Lakeview Inn. Several Bible study friends, a handful of classmates from her seminary classes, and some of Jake's friends from high school, all grown up.

Jake stood near the end of the line, hands shoved in his shorts pockets. She laughed outright and covered her mouth. "I thought you couldn't come?"

He looked sufficiently chastened. "I'm really sorry I had to lie to you."

She gave him a hug and he tried to ruffle her hair, but she shoved him backward with another laugh. At least he had a smile on his face. "Are you going to tell me what's going on?"

He grinned. "Can't say."

Ethan and Lillian approached, and each gave her a hug.

"I don't understand what's going on," she said in between hugs. "What is all this?"

"It was Renee's idea." Ethan backed away and Renee came running. She threw her arms around Jocelyn's neck.

Jocelyn's eyes burned. Still in a state of shock, she held Renee by the shoulders. "Please, tell me what's going on. Why would you plan a surprise party for me on your birthday? Mine was months ago."

She flashed a mischievous grin. "Really, I'm flattered everyone thinks I came up with all this, but I didn't." She stepped to the side and Jocelyn's breath caught in her lungs.

Dylan stood in the glowing light of the restaurant's doorway, a wide and joyous grin on his face, underneath that full beard she'd come to adore. She ran into his arms and buried her face in his chest.

His deep laughter filled her with overwhelming joy. A thousand questions burned, but she couldn't get past the lump forming in her throat. When she glanced up at him, he wiped a tear from her cheek, and then another. "Tell me those are happy tears."

"You're not supposed to be here," she managed. But oh how her heart leapt and somersaulted with joy.

"I couldn't stay away from you a moment longer." He framed her face in his hands and captured a quick kiss—there had to be fifty people staring at them—then pulled away and fell to one knee.

Was he really about to… Right now? Her vision blurred as he retrieved a small velvet box from his pocket. The crowd fell eerily silent as he spoke.

"Jocelyn Monroe, I've never fallen for anyone faster and harder than I have for you. You've been a Godsend to me, and I can't imagine living the rest of my life without you in it. Will you marry me?"

She wiped her face again, still in a haze. Really, was this truly happening? "But … weren't you supposed to be …"

He smiled a tender and gentle smile. "I'll tell you all about

Uganda and about why I'm here and not there, but first you have to answer the question."

She could hardly see in front of her. Wiping tears away did nothing but make room for more.

He reached for her hand, his own trembling. "Jocelyn." His tone wavered.

"I think I've been waiting months for you to ask me." She hardly choked out the words before the crowd around them cheered and Dylan slid a beautiful diamond ring onto her finger.

He stood, spun her around and kissed her again, then led her inside. The crowd followed them, some returning to their tables while others stood around talking. There were more people than chairs available, and Jocelyn couldn't imagine how the cafe would feed everyone.

Dylan led her to a corner booth in the back and they sat together—alone, thankfully—despite the din of conversation surrounding them. She rested in the crook of his arm, and he pulled her close enough to caress the top of her head.

She couldn't not stare at the sparkling ring on her finger. How beautiful and gorgeous and perfect! Oh, this was too incredible.

He gently held her hand and traced the ring all the way around. "You know I wanted to propose before I left."

"I wouldn't have minded one bit." She leaned closer into him. Affection expanded within.

"But everything was so uncertain. I waited because I wanted to be absolutely sure of what God wanted me to do first." He entwined his fingers with hers. "About a month into visiting the school in Uganda, Pastor Brigham came to me one night and said, 'You have the gift of teaching,' and I said, 'Well sure, that's why you hired me.' Then he said, 'This is different. It's more than just the ability to teach the gospel or lead a primary school.

You have the gift of teaching others how to lead and how to teach.'"

"What does that mean exactly?"

"He says there is a great need for local native pastors to be taught sound Biblical theology, and how to lead their local congregations. Many local churches are seeking teachers with experience like I have, to teach other native pastors there."

"That's truly amazing." She tipped her face upward and he rewarded her with a kiss. When she pulled away, she studied his thrilled expression. "Wait. Why didn't you tell me any of this sooner?"

He smiled and pushed her hair behind her ears. "I was still trying to figure out what it all meant. Armed with more information and a tentative plan, I knew I wanted to come home and propose first, so I made plans to come home for Ethan's wedding. But I kept most of what I'd learned secret. I couldn't get your hopes up, in case something prevented me from staying in the States."

"This is so exciting, Dylan." She held a hand to his neck. "I can't wait to hear more about it."

"This new direction is nothing like what I initially envisioned." He rested his hand on top of hers. "This is infinitely better. And it's thanks to you—you were the one who pushed me to step out in faith, even when I wanted to run the other way."

She kissed him again and then leaned on his chest and listened to his heartbeat as he talked of all the things he'd seen and heard and learned.

A server appeared with a giant slice of chocolate cake.

Jocelyn eyed Dylan. "You all do know it's not my birthday, right?"

Dylan loaded a spoon with chocolate cake and offered it to her. "Are you really going to decline chocolate cake?" He extended the bite toward her.

She laughed at his obvious intent. "It's not our wedding day yet."

His eyes sparked with intensity. "I can't wait." He held up the spoon in front of her. "Here's to a lifetime of walking with God, together."

No other piece of chocolate cake had ever tasted so sweet.

The End

ACKNOWLEDGMENTS

This setting and the story inspired by it were a team effort, and I couldn't have accomplished this story without all the wonderful Trinity Lakes Romance authors. I fell in love with the setting as much as I fell in love with my characters. Thank you, ladies, for inviting me to join in on this fun endeavor, and for challenging me and encouraging me throughout the entire process.

Thank you to Melissa Dalley for an absolutely stunning cover. I am continually blown away by its picturesque beauty and how well it captures the images of the mountains in my head where the beginning of my story takes place.

If you fell in love with Trinity Lakes like I have, please leave a quick review and don't forget to check out the rest of the Trinity Lakes novels. They're all standalone storylines full of heartwarming romance from some fabulous authors.

ABOUT THE AUTHOR

Sara Beth Williams is a published author of Contemporary Christian romance, an ACFW and CIPA member and freelance writer. She has a background in freelance publicity, blog managing, newspaper journalism and ten years in the field of education. Two of her three novels have been nominated for a Selah Award. A Worthy Heart (2020) and Anchor My Heart (2022). She lives in Northern California with her husband and two daughters. When she's not held hostage by the keyboard, she enjoys playing guitar, reading, gardening, and spending time with her family.

Find out more at www.sarabethwilliams.com

CONNECT WITH SARA BETH WILLIAMS ON SOCIAL MEDIA

www.ingramcontent.com/pod-product-compliance
Lightning Source LLC
Chambersburg PA
CBHW031020160726
47991CB00005B/1801